GW01607528

The Babe in the Wood

Also by Roger Longrigg

Fiction

A HIGH PITCHED BUZZ
SWITCHBOARD
WRONG NUMBER
DAUGHTERS OF MULBERRY
THE PAPER BOATS
LOVE AMONG THE BOTTLES
THE SUN ON THE WATER
THE DESPERATE CRIMINALS
THE JEVINGTON SYSTEM
THEIR PLEASING SPORT

Non-Fiction

THE ARTLESS GAMBLER
THE HISTORY OF HORSE RACING
THE TURF
THE HISTORY OF FOXHUNTING

The Babe in the Wood

ROGER LONGRIGG

London
MICHAEL JOSEPH

First published in Great Britain by Michael Joseph Ltd
52 Bedford Square, London, WC1B 3EF
1976

ISBN 0 7181 1458 2

Printed in Great Britain by
Northumberland Press Ltd, Gateshead, and bound by
Hunter & Foulis Ltd, Edinburgh

CHAPTER 1

Having a romp with Alicia Spurgeon could be a good idea or a bad idea. There was something to be said on both sides. She edited a magazine, a circumstance which told heavily in favour of a close relationship. Against this she had a braying laugh and wore thick black-rimmed spectacles. She was someone Timothy Barnes wanted to be seen with, but only by people who knew who she was. Many people did not know. Alicia herself did not go about being a celebrity. She did not expect to be recognised everywhere. Her photograph was not heavily featured in her own magazine, and never appeared elsewhere; she was not asked to join television panel games. People were impressed when told who she was, but they had to be told. Ideally, taking her or being taken by her to public places, Timothy would have liked to display a placard identifying Alicia as an important and formidably clever figure in journalism. This not being polite, he tried to limit the public manifestations of his affair with her to places where she would be recognised, such as Covent Garden, or he would not, such as the Ritz.

'Romp' was her word. Timothy approved of it, as emphasising the merry physical side rather than the knotted emotions. Alicia might go in for the knotted emotions—all sorts of people did—but her choice of the word 'romp' suggested that she did not intend them with Timothy. It was a jolly friendship with a plus. She was a fine big lady. Timothy was quite a fine gentleman too, though not big. He was medium-sized, tending to plumpness. His hair was sandy and his skin caught the sun. As a schoolboy he had suffered quite badly from spots but at thirty-five he had almost entirely outgrown them.

Timothy had been married once, Alicia twice. Neither was married at the time when they embarked on their romp. Timothy's marriage had been an error, not gross, speedily put right. Children had not been planned and had not appeared. Timothy's wife had not been put off matrimony: she had married again, at once, with apparent pleasure, and had remained married. Timothy had been put off the whole thing for a bit, but had lately begun to wonder if his life were not lonely and pointless. Meanwhile he lived economically. It was his bachelor life—not lavish but by no means comfortless—which enabled him to be a full-time professional writer. With a wife and brats he would need a lot more money and perhaps even a job. He said 'brats' to himself to lessen the risk of acquiring them, to which, in an access of loneliness, he might suddenly find himself committed.

Romps were safer and much cheaper.

Timothy was not cynical. His success as a writer, such as it was, was firmly based, as plant in soil, on his genuine affection for human beings and his interest in them. Many people had said so, including influential critics and his own literary agent. He knew it to be true. Alicia was not a cynic either, although her marriages had soured her about marriage.

An early result of the romp was that Alicia asked Timothy to write a story for her magazine. She said they printed very few stories by men and those few were of the highest class. She said she was neither simply conferring a favour, nor simply asking for one, but both.

Timothy played the idea cool. He temporised. When Alicia had left his flat, which she filled, he rang up his agent. His agent said that *Wife & Mother* was a perfectly respectable medium in which to be seen, but they paid badly. Timothy had not liked to ask Alicia about this but he was interested in the information. The agent advised

Timothy to write a story with some chance of becoming the basis of a television play, or even a movie, as well as of sale to Australia.

Alicia renewed the suggestion a day or two later, over dinner, in her flat, which Timothy did not fill. He acquiesced. She kissed him. She said she wanted a *real Barnes*. Timothy wondered which of the many real Barneses she wanted. She said she wanted a love story with action and suspense, a bit of nail-biting and cliff-hanging, and an exotic setting. Timothy demurred at the exotic setting, on account of his agent's advice. But Alicia was firm about the exotic setting, and added that the detail must be authentic.

Timothy agreed that detail should always be authentic.

Weeks passed, turning into months. The romp, as a romp, was intermittent, but at any given moment could have been described as on rather than off. It was natural that Alicia should ask from time to time how the story was progressing.

'How's it coming, love?' she asked.

'Slow but sure,' said Timothy.

He said the same thing to his agent, but he lied. It was slow, all right, but it was not sure. It was so slow that it had not started. When he said yes, he would write such a story as Alicia commissioned, he was in no doubt of his ability to deliver the goods. Barnes the pro. Press the button with the right money and the right stuff would come out.

Unease was a long time growing into desperation, but it grew.

Timothy tried to write a story about love on the deck of a schooner in the South Pacific hit by a typhoon. He found himself rewriting C. S. Forester (situation) and Joseph Conrad (setting). He did not object to plagiarism of two writers whom he so much admired, but the story was no good. It was already no good when only two paragraphs had been written, and they were very short paragraphs because Timothy liked to get a story off the ground quickly. A few wisps of Somerset Maugham drifted in towards the end of the second short paragraph, and Timothy realised that he needed an entirely new idea.

He tried to write a story about the frozen North, on account of watching a television documentary. Love in an igloo. The dog-team has fallen down a crevasse. But he bogged down, or froze, among ice-floes and blubber.

The weeks turned into months and there was a deadline. Romp or no romp, Alicia had a magazine to get to press.

Timothy sat in his flat and chewed his ball-point. It was an ordinary ball-point and the flat was pretty ordinary too. The trouble that afflicted him was that the job was a commission. Romp or no romp, the editor had commissioned him. He had accepted payment of half his fee, the remainder becoming payable on delivery of an acceptable manuscript, such acceptance not to be unreasonably withheld. There was a contract. Timothy had signed it; someone had signed it on behalf of the enormous company which owned *Wife & Mother*. Timothy had a copy of the contract and the company had a copy of the contract. Both copies were clear about the date by which the story had to be delivered, time being of the essence.

Alicia did not nag Timothy, but she came as close to it as romping allowed. She rallied him with not delivering the story, and she also rang up his agent. The agent rang up Timothy. It was not really very important. A short story more or less would not be the making or breaking of Timothy's professional career. But a commission was a commission and Alicia was Alicia, spectacles and all. Timothy had grown quite fond of her. She had great big breasts. She was extremely and genuinely kind. She was thoroughly honest both emotionally and professionally, and she had plenty of guts. She was a good person. Timothy had not realised this all at once but it was borne in upon him. He was impressed and abashed. Alicia stood up to people. She took trouble about people. She leaked money like a colander to the deserving and to the undeserving. She distinguished between them with perfect realism, but a lot of the undeserving got handouts from her because she was full of pity. She was full of hope that the undeserving would come to deserve.

Alicia was the salt of the earth, for all her laugh and her dreadful spectacles and her life in magazine journalism. People said so and they were right. Timothy did not understand why she had chosen so essentially pale and ambiguous a person as himself to romp with. He was not a nasty man or a very dull one, but he was not highly-coloured. He lacked flavour. He lacked glamour. He knew this and regretted it. He found that he was a figure of glamour to a few people whom he met in the country, when he spent weekends in the country with married friends: but these people thought it was glamorous to be a writer: that was all: it was the word: it was not Timothy himself: closer acquaintance disabused them: they learned quickly what he had long known, which was that membership of a glamorous trade or profession did not, of itself, invest the member with glamour. Witness actors, explorers, test-pilots, cabinet ministers. The country people who started by thinking he was glamorous because he was a writer ended (after dinner) by thinking that he was nice-mannered and a bit shy and a bit too anxious to please; when, pressed, he told them the names of his books there was general embarrassment because nobody had heard of them.

They were not bad books. Alicia, in certain moods, said they were marvellous, and influential critics said they were rooted, as plant in soil, in his evident and kindly concern with people. They were a bit satirical but they were not nasty. There were four of them. There were also some screenplays and television plays to his credit. They were rooted in what producers and script-editors told him to do.

Sometimes Timothy thought he was a celebrity and sometimes he thought he was an abject nobody. It depended whom he had been talking to. Sometimes he thought he was a good writer with a distinct and personal vision, and sometimes he thought he was a hack. He knew his books were quite good, but he was not really pleased with them because he knew that other people had written closely similar but much better ones. He knew that his screenplays were no good at all, but he was not entirely to blame.

Timothy's hair was quite short owing to his being thirty-five and having thin sandy hair. Several of his contemporaries had grown their hair long, but Timothy thought they were aping youth in an undignified way. Some were fortunate in thick hair; those with hair as thin as Timothy's looked moth-eaten. He often wore a collar and tie, but he sometimes went out to lunch in a turtle-neck if it was that kind of lunch. His parents had been dead for a long time. The aunt who had brought him up, on sound conventional lines and at great expense, was alive but gaga and in a home. Timothy visited her but not often: it benefited his conscience but not her, as she confused him with her own Uncle Timothy, a raffish manufacturer of blankets, who had died in an alcoholic stupor in 1937. Aunt Gloria's conversation distressed Timothy and exhausted her, and the matron said that he was not to come often. It was sad, after all she had done for him, that he could do so little in return. At least she had plenty of money for her comforts, although the capital was diminishing with each hour that she spent in the home. Timothy was her heir, but it was an aspect he tried not to think about.

'Hit it, boy,' said Alicia.

It was her way of reminding him that the story was due in four days.

She arose from his bed like an inflated Venus; one looked for mooring-ropes and cheering crowds.

She went away and Timothy tried to hit it.

He brooded about the Arabian desert (authentic detail from Doughty and Lawrence); the American West (Zane Grey and Matt Chisholm); distant planets (Ray Bradbury and Isaac Asimov). He brooded about love. *Wife & Mother* required happy endings. Timothy himself preferred them. They were not true to life, but that was no great matter to a pro whose button had been pressed. Timothy sought for a love story, any love story, which he could place where he liked. A love story set as it might be in London, but transported by the magic of his imagination to an exotic setting replete with authentic detail. Timothy sought in his own experience. Him and his wife? Him and Alicia? There was precious little else. He sought in the experiences of his friends. Those that had happy endings were devoid of incident. Some of Timothy's friends met girls, loved them, married them, and that seemed to be it. The more interesting histories of other friends did not have happy endings. That was why they were interesting. Tragedy was inbuilt in the situations. Tension and suspense derived from conflict. Conflict was good stuff for drama but not for happy endings. Timothy's novels handled the whole area in a way people found adequate, but they were wry (though deeply human) and had equivocal and downbeat endings. The readers of *Wife & Mother* wanted clear indications of a future strewn with roses. Alicia said this deprecatingly, as though in mockery of her readers, but it was part of the brief.

The way to achieve a happy ending after a suspenseful middle was to use one of the well-tried literary-dramatic devices. Misunderstanding. Mistaken identity. All cleared up in the face of imminent peril. It was a graft job: the plot of *Figaro* in a John Buchan setting, the plot of *Götterdämmerung* in an Alistair MacLean setting. They loved each other but Antic Fate had taken a part in the game. Or a villain had thrown a spanner in the works. *Othello* in a Jack London setting. But with a happy ending.

On this profoundly professional basis Timothy planned his story.

The man pretty hard-bitten. A bloke who had knocked about a bit. Seemed cynical to strangers (as might Timothy himself). Girl believes him to be immune to love, listens to advice to this effect, hears stories, which contain element of truth, about ruthless episodes in the past. He, for his part, believes her to be engaged to worthy young doctor who needs her. He has overheard conversation between old codgers, got hold of wrong end of stick, actually it's her *sister* who is engaged to worthy young doctor who needs her. Possible to do all this without being novelettish by means of a certain acerbity of style.

What happens? The what depends on the where. Avalanche? Man-eating shark? The light aircraft out of control over the volcano? Something of the kind. Revelations consequently blurted out. The moments left to us. All made plain. Then miraculous rescue. Future strewn with roses. All still saved from saccharine by a certain wryness. Style renders it real Barnes. Edge to dialogue, as praised by influential critics. Codgers (marginal characters) provide opportunity for satire, comedy.

All that remains is to find exotic setting, physical threat.

Timothy went out to dinner in a mood of optimism.

He went to a terribly dull dinner party.

He found himself after dinner with a drab man and a pretty drab woman. He did not know their names nor they his. They did not know he was a writer. They did not talk to him but to each other. The woman asked the man whether he had had an enjoyable holiday in Kenya. He enumerated the animals he had seen and photographed. It was an impressive list but the recital of it was dull because he was such a dull man. He said that a friend of his met a man who had an interesting experience. The man took delivery of a new car. On the very day of collecting it he started driving from Nairobi to Mombasa. The car became overheated. It boiled. This was due to a mechanical defect. The man opened the front of the car to let it cool off, and went a short distance away to sit in the shade of a tree. His intention was to wait there quietly until his car had cooled. An elephant appeared. The man sat very still because he knew a thing or two. He was an old hand. The elephant investigated the car. It extended its trunk into the engine, which was uncovered by the open bonnet. The tip of its trunk encountered the cylinder head, which was hot. Infuriated, the elephant set about the car. It turned it over with its tusks and then knelt on it. It trampled it, trumpeting with rage owing to its sore nose. The man, whose pride and joy the car had been, sat watching, unable to move. Movement would have attracted the elephant, which was very angry. The man had to sit still and watch his beloved and very expensive new car flattened to a depth of a few inches.

The drab woman ate up this story. It was the most fascinating thing she had ever heard. It enabled her to produce stories of her own, to which, in reciprocity, the man with the elephant story had to listen. Timothy had to listen to them too, there being no part of the room to which he could move without rudeness. The woman's stories were no good at all. The elephant story was not very good either, Timothy thought, as delivered in the man's monotonous voice.

But when Timothy went home he thought about the story and decided that, after all, it was rather a good one. The elephant, full of innocent curiosity, amiably exploring the inside of the car with the delicate tip of its trunk.

The sudden and awful pain. The elephant's insensate rage at this betrayal. The total destruction of the car, strewn all over the road, flattened as though by a titanic mangle. The awful power of the elephant. Its resistless weight. A creature so strong that it had no natural enemies, that it approached a strange car in a spirit of tolerant friendliness. And throughout the remorseless destruction of the precious car, its owner compelled to sit watching, not daring to move. Yes, it was a good story. Told by the right person it could be a terrific story.

Timothy realised that he was the right person and that the problem of his own story was solved. The drab man had supplied detail. Hemingway would supply more. There would be other animal noises, the screaming of birds and monkeys, the neighing (perhaps) of zebra and giraffe, the grunts of the larger predators. There were snakes and scorpions, ostriches, baboons. There might be naked tribesmen with long spears and secret faces. They drove, the two of them, in the new car, strangely silent. She had been warned about him; he had overheard the misleading conversation. Both loved, neither spoke. The car boiled. All else followed.

Timothy set to work at once. Beside him lay *The Snows of Kilimanjaro* and a postcard of the Mount Kenya Safari Club which a journalist friend had boastfully sent him. He worked until four o'clock, writing straight on to the typewriter, which he rarely did owing to lack of confidence. The story was a little long. He thought it would do.

His agent also thought it would do and Alicia said it would do. Alicia was not wild about it. She said the characters were out of Rider Haggard. Timothy had not thought of Rider Haggard, so this was a bit wounding. Alicia saw that he was upset by her shaft, so she softened it. She said the man was out of Sapper and the girl out of the stories she usually printed. Timothy was not mollified. But he was paid. The story duly appeared with a vivid full-page illustration. The illustration showed an Indian elephant because the artist had been badly briefed. The mistake was not widely noticed by the readers of *Wife & Mother*. Timothy's agent tried to sell the story as a basis for film or television, but without success.

After the publication of the story, but not because of it, Alicia came to be in love with Timothy. This surprised both of them and it was most unfortunate. They agreed that they should stop seeing each other, but the habit was too strong. Alicia wanted Timothy with her all the time, and he wanted her with him some of the time because of her goodness and because she was a fine figure of a woman. She sometimes cried, which was very distressing to Timothy. A large lady has as much right to grief as a small one, but it does not look so good. Timothy found this an interesting and poignant thought; after he had made a copious note of it he remembered that Jane Austen had covered the subject in *Persuasion*. He kept the note because he was not ashamed of agreeing with Jane Austen. He did not show the note to Alicia or discuss its contents with her. He was not asked to write another story for *Wife & Mother*, although they often talked about his career. These conversations alerted Timothy to the possibility that Alicia was planning to marry him. She was the salt of the earth but he did not want to marry her. The idea was grotesque, on account of her size. It was all very sad.

Timothy's career, in spite of these discussions, was rather at a standstill. He did not know where he was going next. He began another novel but he was not pleased with it. The plot was *The Seagull* updated. It worked all right at a technical level, but the effort to take the characters away from the original made them unreal. It was worth going on with only because he had nothing better to do.

His agent rang up and said that he should meet, for

lunch, that day, a man named Euan Crombie. Euan Crombie was an independent film and television producer with respectable credits. He was, even at this moment, en route from Africa. The lunch-date was the result of a series of cables and of telephone conversations with a secretary in Nairobi which had gone on most of the night. The agent was too tired, because of the conversations, to join them for lunch. He did not know what Euan Crombie wanted to discuss with Timothy. It might be an educational film or a documentary. At worst it was a free lunch.

'Of course I've heard of him,' said Alicia. 'I'd like to meet him myself. Perhaps later on you might fix that. I believe he's amazing.'

He was amazing.

CHAPTER 2

Euan Crombie was very tall. He topped Timothy by six inches and Timothy was not a dwarf. He was very thin. He had a mane of hair, streaked with grey, which he pushed back from his brow without bothering further. Most aging men with manes of hair (in Timothy's experience) were terribly concerned about it, however much they pretended differently. But Euan Crombie seemed, like a lion, to have a mane because he lacked a barber. When his hair fell forward over his temples he pushed it back without irritation or self-consciousness. It was very clean hair.

His face was brown and close shaven. If he had shaved on the aeroplane he had made a good job of it. His brown skin was stretched tight over high cheek-bones and a broad, bony jaw. His teeth were irregular but white. His eyes were pale grey and surrounded by wrinkles, although the rest of his face was smooth. Timothy thought he was fifty, but the clarity of his eyes and skin belonged to a younger man.

Timothy had put on a tie and a suit of muted checks. He was glad he had done so because Euan Crombie was very well dressed. He wore an Old Etonian tie. He went to a good tailor and shirtmaker and his shoes were good. They were better than Timothy's shoes, which were suède of a kind falsely alleged to improve with age and brushing. Everything about Euan Crombie was expensive, nothing ostentatious. In spite of his lack of ostentation, he commanded immediate attention because of his height and his mane of hair.

They met in the bar of a famous hotel. Timothy had not

often been there. It was a bit beyond him. He made contact with Euan Crombie without difficulty; Mr Crombie was well known in the hotel. They shook hands. Euan Crombie's grip was firm and dry, but without the bone-cracking exaggeration with which very healthy men sometimes torture the people they meet.

'It's extremely good of you to meet me at such short notice, Mr Barnes.'

'Not at all.'

'Come along.'

Euan Crombie piloted Timothy to the bar.

He said, 'The fact that I no longer myself drink should not dissuade you from having whatever you like.'

His voice was precise, almost pedantic, rather high: not shrill or emasculate, but a pleasing tenor. It went with one part of his apparent personality but not with another: with his expensive clothes, but not with his tanned athleticism.

The barman said, 'Mr Crombie, sir! What a nice surprise. Long time no see.'

'Good morning, George. Six years, I think.'

'Fully that, sir. Every day of six years.'

Timothy found it remarkable that anybody could be remembered by a busy London barman after six years. He himself was forgotten by barmen after six minutes. Euan Crombie was a lot taller than Timothy and had a mane of hair, but there was obviously more to it than that.

Timothy wanted gin: at least two gins and tonics: it was the way he felt. But he was abashed by Euan Crombie's shoes and hair, and by the fact that he did not drink, and by the fact that the barman knew his name after six years. He asked for La Ina.

'A very good sherry,' said Euan Crombie, 'and the one I give to my own friends. But I seriously put it to you, Mr Barnes, that you would really prefer a glass of gin, and are requesting sherry because gin seems the grosser liquor to drink in the presence of an abstainer.'

Timothy blushed. He had been seen through, with ease and accuracy, by a total stranger.

Euan Crombie smiled with great warmth and charm. 'Have a stiff gin and tonic, Mr Barnes, and then another, and then we'll have lunch.'

Timothy smiled back. It was impossible not to do so. He enjoyed his gin and tonic and Euan Crombie appeared to enjoy his enjoyment.

Euan Crombie looked round the bar, which was painted with murals depicting early aviation; the style fell awkwardly between Feliks Topolski and Anna Zinkeisen. Alicia had told Timothy that these were what the style fell awkwardly between, and he accepted that it was so.

Euan Crombie said, 'I have never admired these decorations. I knew the painter extremely well and I was so glad when he was given this job. But he was very untalented. His pictures were not only derivative but derived from ill-chosen models. Not bad models, but ones he was incompetent to imitate. He died under remarkable circumstances.'

'Oh,' said Timothy, who wanted to get to business.

'After twenty years of contented homosexuality, he fell in love with a girl in a circus. He had been persuaded by some ill-wisher to do a series of paintings of a circus, in which, no doubt, there would have been an uneasy mixture of Toulouse-Lautrec and Dame Laura Knight. No sooner had he arrived under the big top than he met and was enslaved by a young lady named Cannonball Cora. It was Cora's pride that she was hurled further from the muzzle of a cannon than any other Lithuanian Jewess in circus history. My poor friend's obsession with the creature was such that he, too, introduced himself into the mouth of the cannon.'

'With Cora?'

'No no. There would not have been room. The muzzle

of the weapon was only twenty-two and a half inches in diameter. It was a tight squeeze for the enamoured fool. What he did not know was that Cora was also loved by her loader and gun-aimer, an uncouth but passionate relative of hers who appeared before the public in yellow tights, like Cora herself, and set the match to the breech of the cannon. This person doubled—slightly more than doubled—the charge of explosive when Henry was to make his maiden trajectory. It was not a public occasion, you understand. This incident took place on a patch of barren ground near Grasse.'

'Grasse?'

'The circus was about to play the towns of the Riviera. Henry, of course, was thrown far beyond the predicted target, where persons were waiting with a fireman's net for his retrieval. He smashed into an outcrop of rock. Death was instantaneous, though I'm afraid unsightly. So ended an unpromising career.'

'What an extraordinary story, sir.'

'Hardly credible. Indeed you are wondering whether to believe a word of it.'

Timothy blushed again.

'I had it,' said Euan Crombie, 'from Cora herself, with whom I became extremely friendly. She is still a contact I value. I became an honorary member of her family, which numbered, at the last count, a hundred and twenty-seven people, all of whom were born into the circus and remained loyal to the tradition. One of Cora's brothers was killed by a fall, when drunk, from the high wire. I was partly induced to give up alcohol as a result of his accident, at least while I worked on the high wire myself.'

'While you—'

'I did not become a member of the family as an on-looker, an outsider. It is a rôle I detest playing. I made a fifty-minute documentary about the circus, producing it while appearing as part of the Flying Ferringhis. I would not care to embark on a high wire now. I never did embark on a trapeze. I almost did, but I was too frightened. I was probably a little old. Another of Cora's brothers was trampled to death by an elephant.'

'How horrible.'

'Yes, and entirely avoidable. He was a very silly fellow. That brings me to the subject I wanted to discuss with you, Mr Barnes. We will pursue it the moment you have finished your drink—please don't hurry—and we are sitting comfortably down.'

Timothy gulped down his drink. It was his second. He did not mind gulping it. He glanced at himself, in the looking glass behind the bar, with a wild surmise.

Euan Crombie was led towards a table, but said that he preferred another. Timothy had never asserted himself in a restaurant to such a point: it would not have occurred to him to try to overrule a head waiter. The head waiter did not mind being overruled. On the contrary, he apologised for not remembering that Mr Crombie liked to watch all the people: he said he ought to have remembered although it was fully six years since Mr Crombie had eaten a meal in the restaurant.

They sat down. Euan Crombie, divining Timothy's wishes, ordered him a large and very expensive lunch. His own was pretty large too.

Euan Crombie said, 'When I was in Mogadishu last month I had occasion to visit a dentist.'

'Nothing painful, I hope?'

'It was not a professional visit, at least not in the sense which your kind enquiry suggests. Besides being a dentist my friend is an accomplished hypnotist. I wanted to see if he could hypnotise a snake of mine, which I had been unable to do. He kept me waiting for a little while, his patients pressing upon him with swollen faces. While I waited I looked at such periodicals as his waiting room afforded. To my surprise there was an English magazine of recent date. I saw in it a lurid representation of an Indian elephant demolishing a car. It is possible. I have seen such a thing. Picture my astonishment, however, when I learned from the text that this Indian elephant was somehow loose in the Tsavo National Park in Kenya.'

'Yes, I'm afraid that's true. The artist—'

'I read your story. May I be absolutely frank?'

'Please.'

'I would rather wound a stranger than an old friend, but I would prefer not to wound even a stranger.'

'Please say anything you—'

'What attracted me to your story was not the human element. I am not criticising your characters, nor their emotional predicament—though I might, perhaps, be forgiven for finding something of the derivative in the situation of fond hearts being separated only by misunderstanding? At any rate the persons did not interest me very much. The animal did. I was very much beguiled by your picture (yours, not that of your illustrator) of the elephant's harmless and trustful overtures, his delicate enquiry, being met by the shocking response of red hot metal.'

'Oh good. Thank you very much.'

'How well do you know our friend *Loxodonta africana*?'

'Not frightfully well as a matter of fact.'

'Had we hours ahead of us, Timothy, I would be becomingly modest about my knowledge of the elephant. I would allow you to arrive, by degrees, at the realisation that I really know a great deal about elephant. But as we have only a short time I will economise with what we have. I will tell you that I know more about elephant than any man alive. Alive is a necessary qualification, because there was an African poacher I knew, my first real teacher, who *was* an elephant. He could communicate with each member of a herd, as an individual, by voice and touch, understanding and being understood. That is still beyond me. He became a game warden, and was shortly afterwards run over by a Hindu pastrycook in Nairobi.'

'What a dreadful waste.'

'No. He had lost his nerve. The point I wish to make—hurriedly, because I must go to Los Angeles in a few minutes—is that by accident, design, good fortune, or a miracle of intuitive understanding, you have portrayed the character of the elephant better than I have ever seen it done in print.'

'Thank you very much indeed, Mr Crombie.'

'Euan.'

'Euan.'

'It is another time saver. Since we are to work together we should come to it eventually. Nothing is lost by acceleration.'

'Work together?'

'If you consent. Briefly, my plan is that you should write a screenplay, set in Africa and largely concerning wildlife, on the basis of an outline which I shall send you from Los Angeles. Your agent can tie up the details with my London office. My idea is not based on your story, but the train of thought which produced it started with your story. For this reason I think it proper to buy the rights in the story. Unless your agent is very greedy I see no problem in arriving at a figure.'

'Nor do I,' said Timothy.

'You will have to come to Africa. The whole thing must be written on the spot. You must be aware of the country and you must get to know the animals. Does that interest you at all?'

'Yes. Enormously.'

'I did hope it would. Now I really must go. I'm afraid I have done all the talking, but you understand that I had a good deal to tell you.'

They shook hands. Euan smiled very warmly and

walked out of the restaurant. Not every head turned to watch him go but many heads did.

Timothy said to his agent, 'Of course I'm longing to go.'

'Yes. It sounds fascinating. *Can* you go?'

'Why not?'

'It's no business of mine, but I was referring to personal commitments.'

'I think,' said Timothy, 'it would be a good thing if I went.'

Alicia was not so sure.

Cables were exchanged, then contracts. The deal was not munificent but it was perfectly fair. Euan Crombie's London office was efficient. It was easier for Timothy's agent than many much smaller deals. The first payment due was an option on the magazine story. The second was a third of the screenplay fee, payable on signature of contract. Both were paid promptly without a sign of haggling.

Round and about, during this period, Timothy often mentioned Euan Crombie, partly in order to show off and partly in the hope of getting information. A distant cousin of Timothy's, a sporting banker, had known him at Eton, where he was considered arty. The cousin's mother had known the family in Scotland—well-connected people, she said, with a barrack of a place. Of Euan as a film producer little was known. Neither Timothy's agent nor Alicia added anything to what Timothy knew. Many independent producers were obscure and mysterious characters. Euan was more obscure than most. This was to be explained by his residence in remote places, by his working in the circus and going to the dentist in Mogadishu.

Timothy's tickets arrived. He bought two pairs of

tropical trousers, one khaki and one jungle green.

'Of course it won't be for ever,' said Alicia.

'I hope not,' said Timothy.

Timothy visited his aunt in the home near Bedford. It was a distressing and profitless visit. Afterwards the matron very kindly walked with him to the car he had borrowed, because she knew how concerned he was. She said his aunt's general health was excellent. There was nothing to stop her living for ever. They had all got quite fond of her although she was a difficult patient. She was quite on the spot about little things. Timothy would be surprised. It often gave them a good laugh. Timothy resented the patronising way in which the matron spoke of his aunt, but he thought the old lady was in good hands.

The outline did not arrive from Los Angeles. Euan Crombie was known to have returned to Kenya. No doubt Timothy would get his briefing on the spot.

'Probably better,' people said.

'I'll come and see you off,' said Alicia.

'Oh no.'

'Of course I will.'

She took him to London Airport in her car. It was evening but still light as the month was August. People had told Timothy that February was a much better time to visit Kenya. Several people had succeeded in depressing him about this. Alicia kissed him with desperation, as though she were certain he would be eaten or trampled, or fall in love with a black. She would not come in to the Terminal to have a drink owing to the difficulty about parking the car. She drove away, a big kind lady with black-framed spectacles in an expensive sports car.

Timothy felt that, with this parting, his adventure had begun.

He was wrong. His adventure was a long time beginning, because Alicia had brought him much too early to the airport. He checked in, handing over his unglamorous suitcase and his portable typewriter. He drank many glasses of whisky in a bar presided over by a saucy Irishman. It grew dark outside. A fat Nigerian, over-anxious to make friends, cross-examined Timothy about whisky. Was it fattening? Timothy said that it was, that all alcohol was fattening. The Nigerian wanted to know what alcohol he could drink to make himself thin. He was discouraged by Timothy's reply that there was no such alcohol. He looked at Timothy with a new distrust and Timothy was frightened, for a moment, that he was going to be assaulted. No such incident occurred. The Nigerian went to another part of the bar to bore someone else. Timothy regretted his departure because he felt terribly lonely. He felt frightened. He had often flown, but not to Africa. He was frightened of wild animals and sunstroke and failure. Euan Crombie would be difficult to please.

The flight was called. Timothy joined a crowd as unglamorous as himself. They went for a long walk. Timothy sat down in the aircraft where he was told to. He was brought a damp napkin, offered to him in plastic tongs like those used in inferior restaurants for salad. Timothy did not know what to do with the damp napkin; it filled no need he had or could imagine. They rose into the air. Timothy watched a film. He could make little of it, because of whisky and mixed emotions, and because the sound track was several seconds ahead of the picture.

Euan Crombie met him at the airport. He was attended by a large retinue. Timothy was too hung over and too sleepy to sort out the members of the retinue, but he could see that they were incongruous. They did not fit with Euan. There were several large American girls, with travel-stained bush-shirts and long dirty fair hair, who shouted to each other about where the car was. There was a neat, neat-featured woman of about Alicia's age but half her weight; she was English; she wore her hair in a braid coiled round her head; she looked as though she worked in a bookshop in a small cathedral town. There were some children. They were all very friendly to Timothy, but at odds among themselves. A quarrel among the American girls had evidently preceded his arrival; it continued with scarcely an interruption while they were all introduced to him, and while they went to the car. Only Euan's great height prevented him from being engulfed by this strange entourage. Timothy was engulfed; he was surrounded, as though by police, and carried to the car.

The biggest girl got behind the wheel of a battered Land Rover. Two other girls climbed into the front beside her. Timothy, Euan, the neat-faced secretary, and an uncertain number of children climbed into the rear parts of the car.

The Land Rover failed immediately to start. 'I wish to God you'd get a *car*, Euan,' said the girl who was driving, 'and drop this heap down a well.'

The girls beside her defended the Land Rover. Their voices were not unpleasant but they were unnecessarily loud. Their conversation became highly technical. In discussing torque and compression ratios they left Timothy far behind.

Euan caught Timothy's eye; he smiled indulgently. The secretary gave a sharp sniff, as though torque were not a word used before ladies where she came from.

Timothy realised at about this time that the girls were not girls at all but boys. They were American teen-age boys, very large and dirty, with very long and dirty hair. Timothy was aghast at the floater he had almost made. Boys like these would never forgive him if he mistook them for girls, even though, by growing their hair to their shoulders, they occasioned the error. Euan, also, would have looked at him oddly. A writer so imperceptive would hardly command his respect. Timothy would have got off badly on the wrong foot. He was thankful the penny had dropped when it did.

The boy who was driving lit a bent cigarette with a certain defiance as he drove from the airport into Nairobi. He was much too young to smoke. He was much too young to drive, too.

Timothy tried to look out of the windows of the Land Rover in order to get valid first impressions of a new world. He could not see out owing to the number of people in the car. Euan Crombie spoke with fluency about the growth of Nairobi into a large industrial and commercial city, but Timothy took in little of what he said. It was difficult to hear because of the noise of the American boys who, when they disagreed, exchanged insult rather than reasoned argument.

The secretary sat in icy solitude. She achieved solitude even in the overcrowding of the Land Rover. She radiated disapproval, which formed a field-force too massive for the people in the car to penetrate. The American boys did not want to penetrate it. They ignored the secretary. They ignored Euan, Timothy and the children. They were intent on their technical discussion; they shouted at each other without regard for anyone else. They were uncouth. It was not at all what Timothy had expected and he was unnerved.

They took him to an hotel.

The secretary said, 'I am afraid you will not be comfortable. They call it a luxury hotel but it is not my idea of luxury. My Gareth and I, at the Clock Hotel, provided a standard of comfort for our guests which was a revelation to many. They had never, they often said, met anything like it before. It is entirely a matter of personal attention. I am afraid you will not find much personal attention here. They do not really care. All they are interested in is the colour of your money.'

'Or, in this case, my money,' said Euan. To Timothy he said, 'You will need boots, as we shall shortly be going to the Rigu.'

Timothy was led to a room. It was breakfast time but he was too tired for breakfast. He was thankful to be alone. He lay on his bed. He did not sleep, but it was bliss to be disturbed only by the noise of traffic and of vacuum cleaners in the passage. He could not have taken much more of the American boys in a confined space. No doubt Euan would call for him later and they would discuss the project.

CHAPTER 3

Timothy spent a lonely day. He wanted to be made much of, but he was abandoned. He walked round the streets of Nairobi; they were streets. The traffic was heavy and some of the buildings were tall. Many of the people were black, many pink. The hair of the older European women was done in tight waves; their hairdressers were conscientious but untalented. No one smiled at Timothy, greeted him as an intrepid traveller, or recognised him as a celebrated writer.

He found a boot shop and bought boots. This occupied some time but not enough.

He went back to his room and wondered what to do. Tea occurred to him as a way of filling in the time; he ordered it on the telephone. English worked on the hotel telephone; in some ways life was easier than in France.

Tea had no sooner arrived than his telephone rang.

A strong young American voice said, 'Tim? You all set to come out to the house for supper?'

It was only five o'clock, but Timothy said that he was all set. He was not abandoned after all. He would have liked a bath and clean clothes before going out to supper with the intensely elegant Euan Crombie, but he was summoned. No doubt there would be a story conference for two or three hours before he was offered an exquisitely made dry martini; he expected dinner to be tête-à-tête with his producer while they went into the structure of the screenplay and the deeper motivations of the characters.

He went down in the lift and found all the American boys assembled in the foyer of the hotel. Clearer-eyed than in the morning, Timothy saw that there were only four of them, not, as he had imagined, eight or ten. He distinguished the driver, who was the biggest and oldest and wore spectacles unlike Alicia's. The others went down in age, but the ages were unguessable; Timothy knew little about children and nothing about American children. These boys had unbroken voices but an air of adult assurance; even the oldest, the bespectacled driver, had an unbroken voice. This argued that he was thirteen or fourteen at most, but he was big for his age and drove the Land Rover with perfect competence.

The boys were having an argument, but they broke it off to greet Timothy with exuberant friendliness and lead him to the Land Rover. The eldest was driving again; he backed with insolent skill into heavy oncoming traffic, and ground and honked through the city and its unkempt outskirts. Timothy admired the way he drove: he was more careful than he wanted to seem. Two of the other boys sat beside him in the front, one beside Timothy in the back.

'I'm afraid I never got your names straight,' said Timothy to his companion, who wore a baseball mitt on his left hand.

'Yeah? Well, here's how we go.' The baseball player barked out a list of names which were not names. They were words like Hack, Rich, Muck and Fizz. It was not clear to Timothy which of these words belonged to which boy; but his shyness prevented him from asking the baseball player to repeat the list. He had, in the event, made matters worse for himself rather than better, because now he was supposed to know what each boy was called.

He said, 'Where are we going?'

'The *house.*'

'Oh yes. Where is the house?'

It was another mistake. The baseball player said a word, a longer word than any of the alleged names but equally meaningless to Timothy. It was an unmemorable word and

Timothy immediately forgot it. It would be embarrassing now to ask where the house was, as it would be embarrassing to ask what the boys were called. He would seem a nitwit, asking for simple information all over again. Timothy felt that he was getting over his knees in social quicksands, or mud, owing to being dropped among these puzzling Americans. He wondered what the house was, and whose. If Euan Crombie's, what were these boys, and whose? Was the house Euan Crombie's office? Would the secretary be there, radiating disapproval? The immediate future was full of questions; Timothy did not ask any of the questions because he knew he would not understand the answers.

The boys talked to each other and to Timothy. He was astonished that, even in the weakened state of the morning, he could have mistaken them for girls. Only their hair was girlish, and that only in length. In other ways they were strongly masculine. Their movements were masculine, their gestures, the subjects they discussed. Except for the youngest, their faces were strong-featured. Timothy's skin crawled at the thought of the offence he would have given, the derision to which he would have exposed himself, if he had revealed that he thought the boys were girls.

They turned off the road on to a track of bright red dirt, which wound between fields planted with sturdy green bushes. The baseball player said that the bushes were coffee.

'Everybody knows that, dumb-dumb,' piped a boy in front.

'Tim didn't know, did you Tim?'

'No,' said Timothy.

'I'll bet you did know, too, Tim. I'll bet you said that just to make Griz feel good.'

'He did not.'

'He did too.'

The argument about whether Timothy did or did not know that the bushes were coffee joined a simultaneous argument about the colour of the legs of a topi. Timothy was appealed to on the latter issue, but he did not know what a topi was. Meanwhile he had made a small advance. The baseball player was named Griz. Timothy took this to be a name from Central Europe, a Bosnian or Magyar name. Griz wore a hugely loose red sweater with the number 26 on the back, jeans held up by a massive belt, and rubber-soled boots like those used for basketball. His hair was long and red.

They passed several low white buildings with corrugated iron roofs. African children jumped out of the way of the Land Rover. The boys waved to the African children, who waved back.

They turned off the track on to a crunching drive between sad lawns, and stopped in front of a bungalow which needed paint over most of its area and glass in some of its windows. Perhaps Griz had been playing baseball.

The boys jumped out of the Land Rover. Two, shouting incoherently, ran round the house and out of sight. Griz picked up a ball from the grass; he began throwing it into the glove on his left hand. He wound himself up to pitch the ball at the windows of the house, but threw it instead into his hand.

The driver smiled at Timothy with great sweetness.

Timothy said, 'Thank you for the lift.'

'That's okay. See ya.'

The driver strode away briskly, his loose prison clothes of blue cotton flapping about him. He looked very strong; he was large and powerful to have an unbroken voice.

Griz also disappeared round the side of the bungalow, leaving Timothy alone. He climbed slowly out of the Land Rover. Unfamiliar birds screeched in a foreign language from a tall tree with a foreign disease.

Timothy went forlornly towards the house. His heart sank further as he neared it. It looked like a house abandoned for months, perhaps years, occupied only by vagrants with unclean habits. A telephone rang and continued to ring, but there was no one in the house to answer the telephone. Timothy realised that he had been brought to an empty house, as a cruel practical joke, by the American boys, who had now run away. They were hiding, watching him with suppressed, merciless laughter. Soon they would jump into the Land Rover and drive away.

The telephone stopped ringing. No one had answered it; it had stopped because the caller, like Timothy, had found an empty house.

Timothy tried the front door. He was sure it would be locked, but it opened. It opened with difficulty because it fitted badly, but he exerted his strength and won a battle with the door. He found himself in a sort of lobby. There was a profusion of plants in pots, but the plants were dead or dying. No one had watered them because there was no one here to water them.

A glass door faced Timothy. Through it he saw a big, bare room with two cane chairs. In one of the chairs sat Euan Crombie. He was as elegant as in London, but in a different style. Timothy had not noticed his clothes in the confusion and fatigue of the morning, but now he observed and admired them. He wore drill trousers, very clean and beautifully pressed, shiny leather slippers, a buff-coloured open-necked shirt, and over the latter a sort of khaki waistcoat. The effect was tropical yet businesslike, casual yet dressy. Euan's hair was longer than Timothy remembered it, but it was very carefully brushed. He had papers spread on his lap; he was studying them and making notes or corrections with a pen. The telephone was on a small table beside him. He had not heard it ring, so total was his concentration.

Timothy felt a surge of relief and hope. He opened the glass door; it was another struggle and another victory. Metal screamed on metal as he pulled the door open: a foreign scream, like the language of the birds. Euan did not look up; he had not heard the door; his face was remote and studious; he made another note on the type-script on his lap.

Timothy cleared his throat. He did not want to prejudice, by ill-timed importunity, an important relationship. Euan was in the middle of an awesome train of thought; he would attend to Timothy as soon as he could spare attention for him.

The youngest of the American boys came into the room. He was carrying a snake. He left the door open and crossed the room, smiling warmly at Timothy, who smiled back. He went out through another door, which he left open. The two open doors allowed a draught to blow through the room. The draught blew the papers off Euan's lap. Some he successfully caught but others eluded him, flapping to far corners of the room. Timothy picked them up and gave them to Euan.

Euan looked up and saw Timothy. He said, 'Thank you very much, that was most timely and kind. You got here all right. What an absurd remark. It is sometimes said, as you know, that courtesy consists of stating the obvious, which has the virtue of starting no argument, which is not contentious, which does not cause the person addressed to fly into a rage. All the rules of social intercourse originated with such an object: contact with other persons, if not stimulating, is smooth. Fights do not begin. Men observe to each other that it is not raining, that the train is late. There is instant accord. A spirit of unanimity prevails. People will tell you that this illustrates the artificiality of human society, of civilisation. They are quite wrong. Gregarious animals employ a similar ritual. They communicate only to agree. Elephant, baboon, hunting dog, certain of the antelopes. The rules governing their relations with each other are quite as clearly defined as our own and quite as time-consuming. It is a necessary condition of group living. Would it interest you to hear about the ceremony with which a cow elephant introduces her calf to the senior members of the herd? It has never, to my mind, been quite accurately described. The text books are wrong. We must have a long talk about that, in relation to the needs of our story, as about many other things.'

'Good,' said Timothy.

The youngest boy came back into the room without his snake, circled it at speed, and came to rest in front of Euan.

He said, 'Hey, Euan, when do we eat?'

'Do you want to eat?' asked Euan mildly.

'Sure do.'

'I expect it will be ready soon.'

'Hey, it's ready *now*, you know that? You know that, Euan? It's ready *now*. Can we eat now, Euan?'

'It appears,' said Euan with a smile to Timothy, 'that it is time for dinner. I hope you have an appetite after the fatigues of your night and day.'

It was just after six. Timothy did not want to eat. He wanted to drink. He wanted to drink, moderately, for at least two hours, discussing the screenplay he had come to write, and then to eat. He did not say so, but smiled a false smile.

The boy ran from the room, calling the non-names of the other boys. The eldest, who wore spectacles and drove the car, came at once, followed by Griz the red-haired baseball player. The fourth boy was missing. A fifth boy appeared instead, whom Timothy dimly remembered from the morning. He was in the sharpest contrast to the American boys, being in appearance and manner so English as to verge on caricature. He was about eleven. His hair was cut short and parted neatly. He wore a school blazer, a school tie, and grey flannel shorts.

The three American boys were already sitting down when Timothy followed Euan into the dining-room. They appeared to occupy more than three places. Euan sat down at the head of the table, indicating to Timothy a place next to him. The neat-faced secretary came in; she sat down beside Timothy, at whom she barely glanced, and ordered with a gesture the English boy to sit on her other side. She had changed into a severe long dress of navy blue; her hair was now in a loose bun of which the effect, like that of the coil of the morning, was aesthetic but provincial.

A black servant appeared in the door and said something in Swahili to Euan. Euan replied fluently and at length. The servant looked at him with tragic, opaque eyes. One of the American boys said a few words in Swahili to the servant, who grinned and disappeared. He came back quite soon with bowls of soup on a tray. It was good soup, though soup was not what Timothy wanted. The English boy took little prim sips from the side of his spoon; the secretary stared at it and left it alone.

Euan said, across Timothy to his secretary, 'Did you have a good day?'

'Not very,' she replied. She had been contemplating her untouched bowl of soup. She glanced up at Euan as she spoke, her expression fathomless. She returned the stare of her cold blue eyes to the soup. She added, 'There is no talcum powder in the house.'

'It shall be procured,' said Euan. 'Cat can go into Nairobi first thing in the morning.'

'Very well. Life is difficult enough as it is.'

'Indeed, indeed.'

The secretary turned her neat, secret face towards Timothy. She said, 'Do you like Africa, Mr Barnes?'

'I can hardly give an opinion yet,' said Timothy.

'Oh. If you think it will improve on better acquaintance, you are an optimist.'

'I *am* an optimist,' said Timothy.

She looked away from him and returned to contemplation of her soup. An expression of distaste, even hatred, was now perceptible on her face; Timothy did not know if he or the soup had caused it.

The secretary forbade the English boy to eat the next course. It was meat, big pieces of overdone steak. The boy wanted some, but the secretary said that he was to have only vegetables and gravy. She sniffed the gravy and forbade that too. She said it was too rich for him. It appeared that he belonged to, or was the responsibility of, the secretary. He said nothing throughout the meal. Apart from her brief instructions regarding the meat and gravy, the secretary also fell silent.

The American boys received the steak with delight. They had good appetites; their manners, though unconventional, were not revolting.

The fourth boy came in. He seemed to Timothy to be the second oldest, falling between the driver and Griz. The driver was evidently called Cat. Timothy thus had two of them named, improbable as were the names; he soon had another, the newcomer, who wore a tent-like sweater in loose-knit wool with holes in both elbows. The newcomer was greeted as Mal or Mall.

The secretary ate a small amount of her steak: a cubic inch, cut into tiny pieces with obtrusive difficulty. She breathed hard as she chopped; it was the kind of hard breathing which is meant to be heard and to invite enquiry and sympathy.

There were shouts from the boys about rags. The youngest boy replied to the shouts, so it appeared that his name was Rags.

The secretary abandoned her steak. She sighed as though everything was even worse than she expected. She turned to Timothy; she said, 'I am so interested that you describe yourself as an optimist. I also have been an optimist all my life. Hope has carried me through all the bad times. I have had some very bad times. My cross has been heavy. Not everyone would have kept smiling as I have done. I have never forgotten my poor mother's advice, just before she went ahead to the Summerlands, where she awaits me with a smile of ineffable bliss. "Count your blessings," she said. "What blessings, Mumsy?" I asked her. I was low at the time; I counted myself unfortunate. "Ah," cried she, "how many girls have both beauty and talent?" Of course I saw at once that she was right. Nature had been prodigal in bestowing her blessings on me. So, when things look dark and storm-clouds gather, I think of those deathbed words.'

After dinner the secretary and the English boy went off and were not seen again. Timothy followed Euan into the room with the two chairs, and saw that an American boy was sitting in each chair. The other two boys were lying at full length on the floor. Cat, if his name was Cat, was sitting in one chair, Rags in the other. Cat kicked Rags on the shin, then stood up.

'Hey,' said Rags.

'Get up out of that chair, dummy.'

'Why? I got here first.'

'Maybe Tim and Euan want to sit down.'

'Don't dream,' said Euan, 'of moving.' To Timothy he said, 'I reserve this room for my own use during the day. I do not feel entitled to do so in the evening also. Do you think I am too indulgent?'

Timothy did think so; he wanted to sit down. But he shook his head, smiling in reply to Euan's smile.

Griz picked up a transistor radio from a corner. African music filled the room, monotonous but not quite unbearable.

Euan shouted, 'This music is enormously helpful to a proper understanding of the cultural differences between tribes. Anthropologists are only just beginning to realise this. I have never been an academic anthropologist, but the discipline has always interested me. *Nihil humanum*, especially in Africa. I think I can claim to have been the first to point out the difference in the use of quarter-tones as between the northern and southern Maasai. That was in a paper I read at the scientific congress in Managua three years ago. I should add that I have never been an academic musicologist. Alas, interesting as it is, I cannot really enjoy this music.'

'Nor I,' shouted Timothy.

'But my children do.'

'Oh yes?'

'As you see.'

CHAPTER 4

Cat drove Timothy back to his hotel in the Land Rover; Rags, Griz and Mal or Mall came too. They came for the ride; they came out of affection for Timothy and for each other. This was evident to Timothy, and he was touched by it. At the same time it did not much affect their conversation. They had a renewed quarrel in which Timothy was occasionally appealed to.

They dropped him at his hotel. Their farewells were brief but loud.

Timothy said, 'Does Mall have one L or two?'

'One,' said Mal.

'Oh yes. I wondered.' To Cat Timothy said, 'Thank you for the lift.'

'That's okay. It's my job.'

Cat gave him, as before dinner, a broad shy smile of great sweetness. He was very dirty. His spectacles looked dirty. Timothy hoped that they were clean enough to see through, especially for driving at night.

An argument about the whereabouts of roan antelope had already broken out between Griz and Rags before the Land Rover drove away. The boys all nevertheless waved at Timothy and he waved back. He hoped Griz did not have his baseball in the car.

'Cat will drive us, with two of the others. Phyllida and Kenneth, with Rags, will come by aircraft.'

'Right. I'll pack.'

'Have you not done so? Were you not apprised of the arrangements?'

'No. No, I—'

'We shall be with you shortly.'

Timothy hung up the telephone in his hotel room. His breakfast was ordered but had not arrived. He was not dressed or shaved. He hurried into his bathroom. In his haste he cut himself with his razor. The blood flowed from his chin: nothing would staunch it: cold water encouraged it to gush: it spotted the nice clean towels. He planted a large piece of powder-blue lavatory paper on the cut, which had, at last, the effect of stopping the bleeding. The accident slowed him up. He dressed and packed as quickly as possible. His breakfast arrived, but there was no time for breakfast, for pawpaw, egg and coffee.

He went down in the lift with his suitcase and his portable typewriter, and waited for an hour and a half in the foyer of the hotel. Faint with hunger and half mad with anger, he went into the bar beside the foyer and ordered breakfast. The waiter looked at him oddly. Breakfast arrived, identical to the one he had left untasted in his room. The Land Rover drew up. Cat waved. Griz and Mal were beside him, Euan behind. Timothy signed a second chit for his second breakfast, and struggled with his suitcase and typewriter to the Land Rover.

Euan was in a trance, from which he emerged after twenty miles of hard driving. He greeted Timothy with courtly friendliness, as though Timothy had that moment got into the car after being long and eagerly awaited.

Euan said, 'This will be our opportunity for extended discussion.' But he relapsed into trance again. Timothy would have liked to relapse into trance, but the bouncing of the Land Rover made such a thing impossible for a person of inferior spiritual discipline.

Timothy looked instead out of a window. They were in a dry vastness. Tall hills loomed at immense distances. No lions or elephants were visible from the window of the Land Rover. The road was good for a time but it became bad. It was almost intolerable to sit in the back of the Land Rover and bounce like a pea in a drum: it was bad on an empty stomach but Timothy recognised that it would have been worse on a full one.

'That Dieter in back?' asked Cat.

'Naw. That's a Toyota.'

'Rover, dumb-dumb.'

'Toyota, you big jerk.'

They argued about the make of vehicle behind them; they relied on speculation rather than observation, since the vehicle was a long way behind and only intermittently visible owing to the dust they were themselves making.

'Dieter is supposed to come along in back of us.'

'He's probably ahead, you were so goddam late.'

They argued about whose fault it was that they had started late.

'It was Euan's fault,' said Griz.

Agreement was suddenly achieved. The boys attained that unanimity, that peace, which in Euan's own analysis was the result of stating the obvious. They obeyed his rules, and those of gregarious animals.

The Land Rover broke down.

It was not drastic: there was no bang or sound of rupture. The engine simply ceased to run.

'I hope Dieter's in back,' said Mal.

But it was not Dieter's vehicle which they had seen far behind. It was not a Land Rover but a Toyota, full of men and women in impressive hats.

'Krauts,' said Griz.

'Krauts. See the guy in the big bush hat with a plastic leopardskin band?'

'Just stinking lousy Krauts.'

Unanimity was again achieved.

They had broken down in the middle of a howling wilderness, on a rough dirt track, with no help visible or likely. Night would fall.

Cat got out to fix the car. Timothy got out too, though unable to help in fixing the car. Cat smiled at him and opened the bonnet of the Land Rover. Mal wandered away in one direction and Griz in another. They did not seem to be frightened of snakes or scorpions. Euan emerged from his trance.

'An electric failure,' he said.

'Gas,' said Cat.

'You will find that I am right. Let us inspect. Are you a technocrat, Timothy? I have been on far too many journeys not to have mastered mechanical engineering. It was that which caused my involvement with motor racing.'

'Oh yes?'

'It happened almost by accident. I was making a documentary about grand prix racing, and was for the purpose at Monza. One of the Ganzarello cars, their new 32-cylinder formula one prototype, was not developing the brake horsepower which the designers expected. I dropped, as it were, the camera, and took up a spanner, or wrench. Thus began an association during which I became their chief tuner and then, for a short time, their second driver. I was considered a little too old to drive a racing car at Monte Carlo or Indianapolis, but I broke the lap record in practice at both places, holding it, on each circuit, for something less than an hour. It is all in the records.'

'Good gracious.'

Euan climbed gracefully from the Land Rover and inspected the engine. He repeated that the failure was electrical.

'Gas,' said Cat.

They began to argue the matter. Cat's manner in arguing with his father was more restrained, in volume and diction, than when he argued with his brothers: but he was quite sure he was right. Euan was equally sure. The conversation became highly technical; Timothy did not understand a word they were saying. He thought it best to saunter away, like Mal and Griz, until peace was restored or the car mended.

An engine could be heard: another approaching car. Timothy climbed a bank and looked back down the dirt road. He was careful not to tread on vipers, adders, cobras or mambas. The vehicle approached slowly, bumping. Behind it was an immense plume of greyish dust. It was a Land Rover. A man and woman sat in it. It stopped behind the disabled Land Rover, over the engine of which Cat was labouring. Cat's hands and arms were black with grease, but Euan had managed to keep himself clean. Cat waved at the newcomers. He climbed under the wheel of Euan's Land Rover and started it. The engine fired and ran. Euan had mended the electrical failure.

Timothy came down the bank to the cars. Mal also returned, from another direction.

Mal said, 'Hi, Dieter. Hi, Renate.'

'Good morning, Mal,' said the woman in the car. The man said nothing, but bowed stiffly over the steering wheel.

'Where did Griz get to?' Cat asked Mal.

'How in hell would I know?'

'You ought to know.'

To Timothy's surprise Mal did not answer. He nodded sourly. Cat pressed the horn of the Land Rover. It blared over the dry and empty plain. Griz did not appear. Cat continued to hoot. Dieter also hooted.

Cat said, 'Ah, heck. Here we go.'

He glanced at Mal. Their faces were worried, and Timothy was infected by their evident alarm. Dieter and Renate looked solemn too. They got out of their car, talking to each other softly in German. They were about Timothy's age, stocky and pale. They looked like brother and sister but their manner was married.

'We will search, all of us,' said Dieter to Cat.

Cat nodded.

'Nonsense,' said Euan. He had appeared to go back into his trance, standing by the front of his Land Rover and staring into the distance.

Dieter and Renate caught each other's eyes and those of Cat and Mal. Shrugging took place, actual or suggested.

'I have myself taught Griz orientation,' said Euan. 'The road runs north west. The child knows that. You are much more likely to get lost in searching than Griz in recovering the road.'

Timothy saw instantly that this was true. His alarm evaporated. It was better to wait by the Land Rovers than to disperse all over the bush.

To Timothy's amazement, however, Cat, Mal, Dieter and Renate set off immediately, in different directions, their faces serious.

'I once found a young colobus monkey who had wandered away from his troop,' said Euan to Timothy. 'On the Tana river, not far from the sea. I kept it under continuous observation for eleven days, filming it and recording its cries. It rejoined its family in the end, using the angle of the shadows of trees to steer it in the correct direction. There is no doubt about this, although I believe I am the only person who knows it. The others had not moved. They were waiting for it, immobile. You understand why?'

'No,' said Timothy.

'Because, had the troop moved, the missing individual would never have found it again.'

Mal, in spite of defying his father and natural precedent, found Griz. He led his brother to the Land Rover. Griz's small, dirty face looked dazed. Mal's manner to him was gentle. Mal put Griz into the Land Rover, then sounded its horn in repeated double toots. This was evidently a signal; Cat, Dieter and Renate responded to it during the next few minutes, trudging back over the semidesert with dust on their clothes and hair.

They got into the Land Rovers and started.

'It was fortunate,' said Euan to Timothy, 'that Cat was not left all alone to diagnose the electrical failure of our motor.'

Griz, recovered, glanced at his brothers. Cat made a face which Griz seemed to understand. They began arguing about the amperage of the batteries of a commercial jet.

They stopped for lunch.

A picnic was produced from the back of Dieter's Land Rover, a Teutonic spread enough for a regiment and just enough for the American boys. Timothy was handed a long crisp roll with slices of cold pork inside. As he was transferring this to his mouth, his knuckles encountered something odd about his chin; he fingered it; he remembered the lavatory paper with which he had stopped his bleeding.

'Lord,' he said. 'I'd forgotten about that.'

'Shaving, Tim?' asked Griz.

'Yes. I cut myself.'

'That's what we figured. But of course we didn't say anything about it.'

'Why not? I would have got rid of it ages ago.'

'If you want to go around with a tissue stuck to your chin, boy, you do it and welcome.' Griz laughed; he had quite got over being lost.

'Paper stuck to his chin?' said Euan. 'God bless my soul, so he has. I had not noticed it.'

Timothy pulled the paper away. In doing so he pulled away the scab which it had helped to form on his chin. The cut began to bleed again.

'Nuts,' said Mal.

Mal went to the back of Euan's Land Rover and pulled out a first aid box. He bathed Timothy's chin with disinfectant and stuck a small piece of cotton wool over the cut. He stopped the bleeding; his touch was gentle.

They stopped in a town for gas for both Land Rovers. The town was all flies and filling stations. Black men in tattered shorts stared apathetically at the Land Rovers; black women carried immense bundles to and fro. Kites flapped about on the lookout for pickings, but Timothy thought the people were too poor to leave any pickings for the birds. It was moderately hot and very dusty.

The German couple came up to Timothy after their Land Rover had been fuelled. They shook hands with him, their manner formal but not hostile.

'Dieter Bruckner,' said Dieter. 'No relation to the composer. He is, by the way, to my mind, a very tedious composer.'

Dieter's English was good but his accent was strong. He looked as though he had very heavy bones. His face was made of some other material than flesh: perhaps suet, perhaps soap.

Renate's face was made of the same material. Her bones were also heavy and she had a wide pelvis.

She said, 'We have heard so much about you from Euan. We are interested to meet a British writer.'

'Of course we have met many British writers,' said Dieter.

'It is always interesting,' said Renate.

'It is sometimes very interesting, sometimes not so interesting,' said Dieter.

'Some writers are very dull,' said Timothy.

Renate looked at him with startled pale blue eyes. 'Is it so? Very dull?'

'My wife is idealist,' said Dieter. He smiled stiffly. Timothy thought he did not intend a stiff smile, in the way of expressing disapproval or dissociation, but the material of which his face was made (perhaps a kind of plastic or hard white rubber) prevented easy movement of the mouth.

Mal shambled over to them from his father's Land Rover. His hands were in the pockets of his jeans and he was chewing gum.

Renate said, 'How is Griz?'

Mal shrugged. 'Snapped out pretty fast.'

'So I thought also. But you should not let Griz go off alone. At home maybe but not out here.'

Mal swore for a short time. He said, 'We can't coddle the kid every minute of the day.'

'We understand that,' said Dieter. 'We have seen. Griz gets mad, being watched all the time.'

Renate said, 'If you need, you know, any time ...'

'Sure,' said Mal gracelessly. He sauntered away, chewing.

Cat drove the Land Rover away from the pumps. He began sounding its horn. The party re-embussed.

Beyond the town the road deteriorated. It was no longer a road but a track running through an infinity of dry yellow grass, a few boulders, some stunted acacia trees. Timothy saw enormous herds of despondent and misshapen cattle. He thought it amazing that the thin grass could sustain them. There were no visible herdsmen; there was no water.

They went down a long slow slope where the track was barely visible in the yellow grass and dry volcanic dust; they approached a sudden hard edge of dense forest.

'Ecologically diverting,' said Euan. 'Riverine forest and arid plain are the most sharply contrasted natural environments imaginable, yet we can stand with a foot in each. One foot is damp and cool and in the midst of one ecosystem, the other is hot and dry and in the midst of another ecosystem. Some species never, by any chance, desert the one environment for the other. This is accepted but not usually explained. Look—we can see thousands of wildebeest, hundreds of topi, dozens of Thomson's gazelle, impala, a few bushbuck—'

'Can we?' said Timothy, greatly surprised and interested. He observed that the throngs of cows were in fact representatives of teeming African wildlife. Griz identified the species for him, although his brothers were convinced that this was unnecessary. Timothy was pleased to find out, without having to ask, what a topi was. He looked at the animals through binoculars, but they were no help to him owing to the bumping of the Land Rover.

The track ran along the edge of the forest. Beside the track, 300 yards ahead, stood an immense herd of gigantic elephants. Timothy's heart bounded with fascination and fright.

Mal nodded at the herd, nudging Griz. Griz made an indifferent face. Cat drove on.

Timothy thought they had gone mad. He opened his mouth to shout a warning. His mouth was dry and his heart thudded so that he was speechless.

The herd consisted of eight or nine elephants. Some were calves, no bigger than ordinary large houses, but the others were as big as ocean liners, as cathedrals. Huge scythes of ivory curved down each side of their trunks. They would turn over the Land Rover with their trunks and kneel and trample. Help was far behind because Dieter was avoiding their dust.

Timothy managed a small, gargling cry.

Griz turned to look at him. He said, 'How's the jaw, Tim? Did Mal fix you okay?'

Cat slowed as they neared the elephants. He slowed to a walking pace. They got nearer and nearer.

An elephant on the edge of the herd looked at them steadfastly. Timothy recognised it as an old bull, the king of the herd, its defender. It would trumpet and charge.

'Alicia!' cried Timothy as a kind of prayer, as an invocation of the normal.

Cat stopped the Land Rover. They were very near the elephants.

'How come?' asked Mal.

'I didn't stop, dumb-dumb. The heap died on me.'

'A renewed electrical malfunction?' said Euan, waking up.

'Gas,' said Cat.

'Your story re-enacted, Timothy. How do you cast us for the rôles in your little drama?'

The immense bull elephant was in no doubt about how he was cast; he was the destroyer, the scourge of vehicles and of people. He began to move towards the Land Rover with the inexorability of a dynamited skyscraper teetering from its foundations and committed to immeasurable havoc.

CHAPTER 5

'Alicia's a cute name for that little cow there,' said Griz.

The elephant came a few paces towards the Land Rover. She stopped. She turned round and went away again. She rejoined the others under the trees at the edge of the forest. She was female, quite young and small: Euan said so: Timothy accepted his ruling in the matter.

Cat and Euan got out of the Land Rover. Timothy did not care to do so; he was not confident that his legs would support him. Cat buried his head and arms in the entrails of the Land Rover; Euan watched him with approval and with a flow of technical language. By dint of following Euan's instructions, Cat mended the car. It started and they drove on. The elephants ignored them. Timothy found that his hands were still shaking but that he could almost control his voice.

The track became very bumpy and muddy. It led them at last to a clearing in the forest on the bank of a large brown river. Timothy knew that the river was called the Rigu; it was uninviting; it was said to teem with crocodile and hippopotamus. There were buildings of various sizes by the river; smaller buildings with thatched roofs were visible further along the bank. This, Timothy was told, was the Rigu River Game Lodge. It resembled not a lodge but an unplanned and impoverished village. A few Land Rovers and Toyotas were parked, among which a dozen people wandered in a wide variety of clothes. Some were the Germans who had passed them on the road; they were dressed as though for a long journey on foot in appalling conditions. Others, including three girls whom Timothy took to be Swedish, were dressed for a cocktail party, although it was not much after tea time. The people were under-employed. No one was amusing them. They were staring at the parked cars without looking at them. When Cat stopped his father's Land Rover they surrounded it at once as though taking its occupants prisoner.

Timothy got out of the Land Rover. His legs worked, but not very well. A man came up and shook hands with Timothy. His grip was cruelly hard. He said his name was Bill; Timothy had no difficulty in believing this. Bill greeted Euan and the boys as old friends. The boys returned his greeting but Euan did not notice it.

Bill said, 'Mrs Morgan-Evans got here all right with the nippers.'

Mal swore softly but at unusual length.

'Good, good,' said Euan. 'Where are they now?'

'She went to rest. We offered her some tea, but she said she preferred to lie down. She took the kiddie with her.'

'Kenneth,' said Euan.

'Oh yes? I don't think we've ever had a Kenneth here. I don't know why. It's not a rare name. I've known a good few Kenneths in my time. Curious that. Mollie, have we ever had a Kenneth here?'

'What an extraordinary question,' said a woman with a tragic face.

'Why? Why is it extraordinary? I don't see why it's extraordinary. What's so extraordinary about asking if we've ever had a Kenneth here? However if you won't help me you won't. Now you must all sign the register if you don't mind.'

The register was on a trestle table in the nearest hut. The hut was an office. It was difficult to move about or talk, because the people who had been wandering about amongst the cars now took to wandering amongst the filing cabinets of the office. It had become the scene of the action. A flicker of animation crossed a few faces, and cigarettes were lit with an air of suppressed excitement.

Timothy signed the register last. He saw the cramped, back-sloping hand of Phyllida Morgan-Evans, the round and unformed script of Kenneth Morgan-Evans, the dashing fist of Rags Crombie, Euan's academic italic (very legible, with a Greek E at the end of Crombie) and the marks, made as though by twigs or bones, of Cat, Mal and Griz.

'Capital!' said Bill. He was about Euan's age, plump and red-cheeked. His clothes were also like Euan's, but he had put on a lot of weight since acquiring them: or perhaps they had been left behind by a visitor to the Lodge, a slim man either forgetful or in default of his bill.

'Why capital?' said Mollie. 'All they've done is signed their names. What's capital about that?' She spoke from the middle of the crowd of people who had come into the hut to be amused.

'I believe there *was* a bloke called Kenneth,' said Bill. 'Or Kevin. It might have been that. Some months ago. I'll look it up presently. I like to be clear about things.'

The newcomers were led to their cabins by black men in boy scout uniforms. The men carried the luggage. Timothy's man dropped his typewriter. Timothy was very angry, but he thought it best to get to know his way around a bit before blowing his top.

Timothy had a cabin to himself, at the top of the steep bank of the river. He understood that it was called a banda. Next to him was Euan, also alone. On the other side were Cat and Rags, and beyond them Mal and Griz. Mrs Morgan-Evans and her son were beyond Euan; it seemed they were still resting, as no signs of life came from their banda although the younger Crombie boys surged round it arguing passionately about vultures. They seemed pleased to see each other again. No doubt Mrs Morgan-Evans would take up her secretarial duties when she had sufficiently recovered from her journey.

Timothy's boy scout hung about in the banda after

putting down the suitcase and the typewriter. Timothy took out his handkerchief and wiped the case of the typewriter where it had struck the ground. He thought this would be at once a reproof and an excuse not to tip the boy scout. He was not mean about tipping but he was ignorant of the local scale: in the hotel in Nairobi he had both grossly overtipped and miserably undertipped, judging by the response, and this had made him feel shy.

The boy scout watched him rub the typewriter-case with his handkerchief. He showed no signs of going away. The position was becoming ridiculous. Every speck of dust had long since been rubbed off the case. Suddenly the boy scout burst into a torrent of speech; he snatched the handkerchief from Timothy and himself began to polish the typewriter-case with furious energy. He polished not only the part which had hit the ground, but all the rest too; he went carefully under the handle and paid particular attention to the hinges.

Beyond the office hut there was a bar hut. Its exterior was featureless, even grim, but inside it was gay with pictures. The largest picture was an official portrait, brightly reproduced, of the President of the Republic, with fly-whisk and funny hat. All the other pictures were of animals and birds, original oils, unframed, over-careful but not incompetent, signed Mollie McDavitt. The barman was another boy scout, but of higher rank.

Timothy considered a drink. He did not want a drink yet, not alone, but he wanted *something* to do. After a day of togetherness he felt abandoned again. The others had all disappeared into their bandas; even the Crombie boys were silent. Timothy had lingered in his own banda, after overtipping his boy scout for polishing the typewriter-case; he had unpacked his suitcase as slowly as possible, but twelve minutes was the most the job could be made to last.

He decided against a drink, for the moment. He was in doubt about who paid for his drinks. His contract with Euan stipulated that the latter paid Timothy's expenses, but drinks might be considered outside this arrangement. It was a question that needed to be explored, especially as the list of prices displayed beside the bar showed that drinks were by no means cheap. Pending exploration, Timothy waved noncommittally to the barman and walked between immense trees to the edge of the river.

The bank was high, a cliff of dried mud. The river swirled by at the foot of the cliff, brown and menacing; neither crocodile nor hippopotamus was visible, but it was easy to imagine them inches below the opaque surface of the water. A boat was tied to a stake at the foot of the cliffs; its bows were in the water but its stern was pulled up on the mud. The boat was to be reached by a steep path. Timothy decided to inspect it. It looked an ordinary boat, a craft of no oddity or other distinction, but inspecting it would bring nearer the time when togetherness would resume. Timothy began to go carefully down the path; the heavy crêpe rubber soles of his fine new Nairobi safari boots gripped the dried mud. He got a third of the way down without incident. At that point a few steps had been let into the path in order to make it more dangerous: the steps were logs and they were slippery. Timothy's feet shot out from under him when he lowered himself on to the first log step; he fell heavily and skidded all the way down the bank into the water. He sat down in the edge of the river, in glutinous mud and eighteen inches of water. He had hurt his back and his side and his left leg. He was very near to tears as he sat, hurt and winded, in the mud and water of the river. Though hard when dry, the mud was extravagantly soft when wet. It clung and sucked when he tried to move. He struggled to his feet but fell forward at once on to his knees, grabbed and inhaled by the soft mud.

The river was full of crocodiles. Griz had said so in the Land Rover and neither of his brothers had raised the smallest objection. It was a river famous for the number and ferocity of its crocodiles. Timothy knew (Griz had told him) that crocodiles pulled their prey under until it drowned, then kept it there until it decomposed. They preferred the flavour of decomposed flesh, or were only able to masticate it decomposed owing to the shape of their teeth, or were only able to digest it decomposed owing to their alimentary arrangements; about this there had been disagreement in the Land Rover. It made little difference to the victim. Terror gave Timothy new strength and resolution. He pulled himself out of the wet mud of the river on to the dry mud of the bank; he pulled himself up the bank a little to be out of reach of the crocodiles.

'Geez,' said a voice far above. 'Look who went for a swim.'

'Hold it right there, boy.'

There was a skidding noise, as of descending buffalo. Timothy's arms were grasped by hands of immense strength. Cat and Mal hoisted him up the bank to the grassy asylum of the top. He found that he was on his feet and able to walk.

'You know what you did?' said Mal. 'You opened that cut on your jaw.'

'You want to get out of those wet clothes,' said Cat.

The clothes were not only wet but also muddy: the whole of his left side, and both his legs to mid-thigh, were encased in red mud, as though he were about to be roasted in the embers of a fire, or a plaster cast taken of him.

'You probably have a few abrasions there,' said Mal. 'I'll go get the Mercurochrome.'

He trotted away towards the Land Rover. Cat went with Timothy to his banda. The evening sun glared almost horizontally through the Lodge; they went in and out of the huge shadows of the tree trunks. The sun was reflected on Cat's spectacles, giving him an inhuman look. His hands and bare forearms were still black from the grease of the Land Rover's engine.

They arrived at Timothy's banda. At the same time Mal trotted up with the first-aid box from the Land Rover.

'I'll start the bath,' said Cat. 'Get those clothes off.'

Cat went into the small annexe to the banda which was its bathroom. He turned on the shower. Water thundered on to the concrete floor.

Timothy struggled out of his muddy clothes. Mal watched him with interest. He threw them, as he removed them, out of the door of the banda. His throwing arm felt weak and inaccurate; his clothes were strewn over a wide area. The local boy scout appeared as though he had been waiting, in hiding, for just such a hail of clothes. He moaned as he picked up the mud-caked clothes.

Griz came into the tent. He had resumed his baseball glove. He whistled when he saw Timothy sitting naked on the edge of his bed. Much of the mud had gone through Timothy's clothes on to his legs and his side, but it did not hide the fact that he had lost some skin and his left knee was bleeding.

Cat came back into the tent. He looked at Timothy with undisguised interest. The interest fought with equally evident embarrassment; interest won; all three boys were staring at Timothy.

Timothy had been at boarding schools from the age of seven to the age of eighteen, and then to Oxford. One or more times a day, in his youth, he had stripped among other boys: in the morning, before and after games, at bedtime. He was surprised by the inspection to which he was now being subjected. He supposed that American boys, attending day-schools, never had the chance to became blasé about nakedness.

Cat, appearing to blush, said that the water was now

hot in the shower. Timothy should get clean before they treated his abrasions.

'He ought to use antiseptic soap,' said Griz.

Rags came into the banda carrying a mongoose. He squatted by Timothy's bed and peered at his injured knee through a curtain of dirty yellow hair.

'He ought to have a shot of anti-tetanus,' said Rags.

'Get in that bath,' said Cat to Timothy.

Euan came into the banda. He was carrying a sheaf of typescript. He scrutinised Timothy's knee and flank.

'What a mischance,' he said. 'I am so sorry. To fall is disagreeable and humiliating, but you have here added injury to insult. Fortunately you are in good hands. Tropical medicine is one of the subjects which circumstances have obliged me to study; I am, as a matter of fact, the only lay member of the Norwegian Institute of Tropical Pathology, an honour as unexpected as it was, though I should hardly say so, deserved. Are you allergic to any of the broad-spectrum antibiotics? I will give you a capsule immediately and another when you retire.'

Mrs Morgan-Evans came into the banda, accompanied by Kenneth. She was dressed for gardening, he for cricket. She hissed sharply, as though at the villain of a melodrama, when she saw Timothy sitting on his bed. She turned her back on him, and obliged Kenneth to turn his back also. She said, 'A weak solution of Dettol in warm water. The open cuts should be covered with a loose gauze bandage. Then you had better go straight to bed.'

Kenneth said, 'I say I'm frightfully sorry, sir, is there anything I can do to help?'

Because of Mrs Morgan-Evans's presence, Timothy reached for and put on his dressing gown. He got stiffly to his feet. He had not spoken since his rescue and he felt incapable of speech.

Cat held the door of the shower open for him. Timothy hobbled past Cat, who grinned at him. He smiled back, an action which, a moment before, he would have supposed impossible. Cat was quite wet from adjusting the temperature of the shower. There were drops of water on his spectacles and on his hair, but the water had not washed away any of the grease from the Land Rover.

Timothy shut the door and tried the temperature of the shower. It was perfect. Cat had unpacked his washing things from the spongebag which Alicia had given him for the journey: his rubber sponge and nail-brush lay beside a bar of soap which Cat had unwrapped. Timothy washed off all the mud without difficulty or severe pain. He found that his injuries were slight. He felt better and better under the influence of hot water and of relief. He did not want any of the treatments which were being prescribed for him. He thought he owed it to Mal to submit to anything he suggested, but he did not want pills or jabs, or to go straight to bed.

He dried himself tenderly with one bath towel and wrapped another round his waist. He hoped that his banda would be less full of people, but he found that it was fuller. It was so full that he could hardly get into it, as Dieter and Renate Bruckner and Bill and Mollie McDavitt had joined the Crombies and the Morgan-Evanses. The boy scout, with an armful of muddy clothes, was also trying to force an entry, but this attempt was thwarted by the broad back of Renate.

'Of course we're covered by insurance, if you should lose a leg or anything,' said Bill. 'Meanwhile I think you rate a jar on the house. What's your poison? Scotch and splash? You look like a Scotch man to me.'

'Antibiotics and alcohol do not mix,' said Mrs Morgan-Evans.

'Iodine,' said Mollie. 'I know you people all think I'm old fashioned. But when all's said and done it's the stuff to give the troops.'

'I think what Mr Barnes needs,' said Renate, 'is to be

left alone in his own rondeval so that he can put on his clothes.'

'First square rondeval *I* ever saw,' said Griz.

'Mercurochrome,' said Mal.

Bill went away, telling Timothy that he expected him, as soon as convenient, for a free gratis beaker of sherbet at the water-hole.

Mollie followed him without a word but with a speaking look.

Euan said, 'I had planned an extended discussion, Timothy, but in view of your injuries I suggest postponing it until after dinner. Does that fit in with your plans? Will you be well enough? You are sure? So be it.'

He went away with his bundle of typescript.

Dieter winked at Timothy. Timothy was amazed, never before having met a German who winked. Dieter stood aside with stiff courtesy for Renate to precede him out of the banda.

Rags said, 'I guess this 'goose should eat.'

The mongoose seemed impatient of being carried, but was offered no choice. Rags took it away.

Griz said, 'Play ball, Mal?'

'Shove off,' said Mal.

Griz nodded and went out. He began hurling a ball into his glove.

Mrs Morgan-Evans said, 'Mr McDavitt's suggestion is quite irresponsible. He should know better. But what can you expect of colonials? But I don't suppose you will pay any attention to my advice.'

Kenneth said, 'Goodbye, sir. I hope you'll soon be better.'

Cat grinned at Timothy. He went to the other bed and sat down on it, sighing. Timothy was glad he did not have to sleep in that bed, as Cat was very dirty and smelled of motor-oil and cheap cigarettes. Cat lay down on the bed, stretching his arms above his head and yawning.

This position enabled Timothy to see that Cat was, after all, a girl. Her style of dress, the huge belts and sweaters and loose prison clothes, normally concealed her figure as to both concavities and convexities. When she lay on her back, with her arms stretched to yawn, her figure was suddenly evident. It was a good figure. This put her face in perspective. It was young and round; the features were strong, but the chin was soft and the nose small. Timothy did not understand how he could have thought her face masculine. She had heavy, straight eyebrows, darker than her hair.

Mal was also a girl. She became feminine not by lying down but by taking the stopper out of the bottle of Mercurochrome. While her ministrations were still in the discussion stage she remained sexless or specifically masculine, but she was a girl as soon as she had the open bottle in one hand and a swab of cotton wool in the other. She appeared to lose many pounds of weight and to redistribute those that remained. She was very like Cat in feature but more sullen in expression.

Cat appeared to go to sleep while Mal anointed Timothy with Mercurochrome. It was an unfamiliar chemical to him: he was startled by its brilliant redness and by the area of his body which Mal painted. She painted him gently. The stuff did not sting badly, and in any case there were not many open wounds even of the shallowest kind. He continued, now alerted, to remain decent while she rubbed him with scarlet paint. She spilled none of the Mercurochrome on the towel or on the bedclothes.

Cat lit a Sportsman cigarette from a battered pack. She did this without opening her eyes. Timothy thought she could see as well with her eyes shut as open, as her spectacles were quite opaque with dirt.

Timothy said, 'What is Dieter?'

'Kraut,' said Mal.

'Yes, but what does he do?'

'Cameraman. Pretty good.'

'And Renate?'

'Assistant. Times she drives, when Dieter has the camera mounted.'

'Times she operates the camera,' said Cat, still without opening her eyes.

'Times she directs.'

'Times *he* directs.'

'Are they filming here now?'

'Sure. Why d'ya think they're here? Why d'ya think *you're* here?'

'I don't know. Nobody's told me. What are they filming?'

'Mostly animals, like always. Today they stopped and shot some footage of that big pride we passed.'

'Pride?'

'Of lions. Twenty-three. Half a mile past those young elephant.'

'Which we passed today? Twenty-three lions?'

'Sure.'

'Oh.'

'Hold *still.*'

'Sorry,' said Timothy.

'Okay. You'll live.'

Cat sat up and looked at him. It appeared that she could see through her spectacles, since she began to laugh at what she saw. Timothy had not heard her laugh before: shout, swear, sing briefly, talk, argue but not laugh. Her laugh was high and unexpected like a little girl's. But she was not a little girl. Timothy thought she was twenty.

She said, 'You look like an Apache with leprosy.'

She stood up, adopting the slouch and the jutting butch jaw of her usual manner.

She said, 'Go have that free drink. It's the last you'll get around here.' She slouched out of the banda.

Mal stoppered up the Mercurochrome and put it in the first-aid box. She picked up the box. She was no longer a girl. Her weight was increased and redistributed. She went out of the banda.

Timothy dressed in his remaining clean clothes. The sun had gone down. It was getting dark quickly and the evening was cool. In spite of the dark and the cold he could hear, while he dressed, that Mal was playing baseball with Griz behind the bandas.

CHAPTER 6

It was almost dark. Reports of the brief tropical twilight were not exaggerated. Mal and Griz had stopped playing baseball. The sky was cloudy; the clouds, just visible, were moving in all sorts of directions. On the plains, very far away, lightning flickered, followed after a long time by unobtrusive thunder. Timothy hurried from his banda towards the bar so as to be caught neither by tropical night nor by tropical storm.

In Euan's banda and in Mrs Morgan-Evans's there were lights. Timothy's banda was equipped with a lamp, but he did not know how to light it. Singing could be heard through Euan's window: a reedy air, and words which were perhaps Gaelic. Some kind of catechism was going on in Mrs Morgan-Evans's quarters: questions in her voice, answers in the boy's. Timothy's curiosity about the catechism was not as great as his desire to get to the bar before he was benighted or struck by lightning.

As he passed the banda beyond Mrs Morgan-Evans's, Renate came out of it. A lamp illuminated its interior; Dieter was visible stacking boxes. Some of the boxes were of silvery metal, some wooden but banded with metal, like the tuckbox Timothy had taken, padlocked against his thieving friends, to his private school; they were of all shapes and sizes and there were a great many of them.

'Dieter's equipment,' said Renate. 'He insists to keep it where we are, but to dress and undress is difficult for us.'

Renate was carrying an umbrella and a flashlight. Timothy took it that she was going for a hike, or nature ramble. He was afraid she would ask him to join her, but instead she said, 'Did Malvina cover you with medications?'

'Yes,' said Timothy. 'She did it very well as far as I could judge.'

Renate nodded. 'It is something she learned from her mother.'

'Who was her mother?'

'She is called Mrs Petersen. Goodbye. Perhaps we shall meet at the evening meal. The food here is excellent. I can strongly recommend the kitchen.'

Bill McDavitt greeted Timothy in the bar, which was already lit by hissing pressure lamps. Timothy wanted a whisky and soda, but he asked for a brandy and ginger because he disliked fulfilling predictions. Bill tried to sell him some, or all, of Mollie's paintings, of which he took Timothy on an extended inspection. The prices were moderate. Timothy explained that he had no money of his own with him, as his expenses were being paid by his employer. Bill laughed and accepted this immediately. He began to tell Timothy about the other people staying at the lodge, the parties of Germans and Swedes; he made them sound delightful and very interesting. Timothy realised that, to Bill, they *were* delightful and interesting: he was a man of good will.

'Of course,' said Bill, 'dear old Euan is the most fascinating bloke of all.'

'I quite agree.'

'You do? You really do?'

'Absolutely.'

'What that chap's done. The things he knows about. I used to think he was rather an odd bird in a way, friendly as anything one minute and doesn't know you from Adam the next. Then I realised. He's *thinking*. I suppose, in your line of country, you have to do a good deal of the same kind of thing, but to a bloke like me it takes a bit of getting used to.'

'A surprising family he has,' said Timothy in cautious enquiry.

'Just what I say,' said Bill. 'You'd never guess he was a marrying man, a family man, father of all those splendid fillies. Grand girls I call them. Liven things up here no end, good for a laugh a minute.'

Bill had not met Mrs Petersen. He understood that she was now married to a dentist.

He had known Dieter and Renate for a couple of years. Dieter was a good scout, a real good egg, as well as a wizard with the camera. Renate was the salt of the earth, do anything for anyone, the best pal you could have in any moment of trouble.

And Mrs Morgan-Evans?

Bill was at once noncommittal. He had heard this and that, from Euan and others, but he had not had a chance to judge for himself. 'In any case old boy, I'm sure you'll agree that it's a bit off if I start gossiping about one guest to another.'

Timothy bought him a drink, signing a chit for what he hoped was Euan's money. But Bill revealed nothing about Mrs Morgan-Evans.

Mollie came into the bar, carrying a flashlight and an umbrella. She refused the offer of a drink from Timothy and the supplemental offer, made with greater evident sincerity, of a drink from Bill.

She brought silence with her. To break it, Timothy said, 'Of course, I can see that Euan needs a secretary.'

'Girl called Olga,' said Bill. 'When I say *girl*. She came here for a few days once.'

'Olga? Came here?'

'Do you know Olga?'

'No. What I was wondering—'

'Of course she's based in Nairobi. A bit of a battleaxe we thought, but you can see she's efficient. She didn't altogether fit in here. I mean, it's such a small place we're just one big happy family, everybody gets matey, but Miss Olga was definitely snooty.'

'But Mrs Morgan-Evans—'

'Back to her, are we? I really can't tell you anything about her at all.'

'I can,' said Mollie, unexpectedly and with venom.

'Yes, old thing, I daresay you can, but what I've been saying to Mr Barnes—or Timothy? Do you mind? Timmy? Tim?'

'Whichever you prefer.'

'Whichever *you* prefer, old boy. We're generally on a first-name basis by the end of the first night's booze-up. What I say is that Euan knows his own business best. His girls need a mother.'

'They've got a mother,' said Mollie.

'Ah, but she's six thousand miles away. Married to a dentist. Not that that makes any difference.'

'She brought them up.'

'Yes, and did a first-rate job too, in my humble opinion. But now they're here. I don't know what Euan's planning about their education.'

'I can't see his fiancée teaching them,' said Mollie.

'Why not?' said Bill. 'She's teaching her own son. She told me so this afternoon before she went to bed. As a matter of fact, I'm not surc they weren't having a lesson just now.'

'Teaching her own son is quite a different thing,' said Mollie.

'Why? Why is it different? What's different about it?'

Mollie did not reply. She went instead to a bookshelf in the corner and began turning the pages of a book as though she hated them all.

A lot of people came into the bar. All carried flashlights and umbrellas. The people were in two parties which had not coalesced into one big happy family. If there was not open hostility between the parties there was certainly mistrust. The garments of the people were as varied as in the afternoon. The party of middle-aged Germans, previously dressed for a foot-safari in the desert, was now ready for the opera; the party of young Swedes, previously ready for cocktails, was now dressed for football or mixed hockey. They all arrived at the bar at the same moment, and required the services of the barman. He was in a predicament with which Timothy sympathised. It was impossible for him to serve the Germans without angering the Swedes, and vice versa. The barman's face had none of the impassivity of black Africa. It was crumpled with worry as the leading German and the leading Swede called at the same moment for drinks for their parties. He was a very unhappy barman in spite of his superior boy scout uniform. It was unbearable to look at him. It was pleasanter to look at the Swedish girls, until they became angry with the barman; then it became unbearable to look at them.

Timothy looked out at the night. It was extremely black. To get back to his quarters he would need a flashlight. Nobody had warned him about this.

The beams of two flashlights wavered towards the bar. Behind them came Euan's fiancée and her son. They had also changed their clothes: they were dressed for school chapel. Mrs Morgan-Evans carried an umbrella. She inclined her head towards Timothy.

Kenneth said, 'Hullo sir.'

His hair was neatly brushed and his school tie lay exactly in the middle of his collar.

Mrs Morgan-Evans went to the bar. She sliced through Germans and Swedes and asked for a large gin and tonic and a Fanta. They were given to her at once. The faces of the Swedes were contorted with rage as they were again baulked of their drinks.

Mrs Morgan-Evans bore her trophies away. She gave

the fizzy orange Fanta to Kenneth, who said, 'Thanks very much, Mum.'

Mrs Morgan-Evans said to Timothy, 'It seems wise to get some protein in this form, as I'm afraid the food is bound to be disgusting.'

She made the remark loud enough for Mollie to hear; it was clear from Mollie's expression that she had heard.

Bill was fratting with the Germans. Winning the race for drinks at the bar had made them bonhomous, and Bill increased their bonhomie. Timothy saw that he did this sort of thing well. But he did not do it too long. He came merrily over to where Timothy was standing with Euan's fiancée and her son.

Bill said, 'I knew there was something on my mind. Something I meant to tell you both. I checked up with the register. There *was* a Kenneth here. Ken we all called him, after a day or two. That's the way we are. You must take us as you find us. He had a beard. I rather think he came originally from Luton.'

'Oh yes,' said Timothy.

'So you see I got it all sorted out in the end. I do, in a funny way. Nobody believes I will, least of all my better half. Now if you'll excuse me I must go and make my salaams to our Swedish friends.'

Mrs Morgan-Evans got herself another large gin and tonic. She said that Kenneth could not have any more fizzy orange because it would spoil his appetite for supper.

Thunder crackled much nearer. Timothy jumped and bit his tongue. Immediately it began to rain; there was a pattering on the iron roof of the bar which grew in a few seconds to a thundering as loud as the thunder.

Kenneth said, 'Aren't you glad I made you bring the brolly, Mum?'

'You did not *make* me bring it, Kim. Boys of your age do not *make* grown-ups do things.'

There was a huge shouting in the rain. Euan's daughters ran into the bar. Cat and Rags shared one umbrella, Malvina and Griz another, but they were nevertheless wet. Cat's spectacles were again covered with drops of water. None of the girls had changed. Cat had not attempted to get the grease off her hands and arms: or, if she had tried, she had failed. She and Malvina collapsed their umbrellas at the same moment. Water showered from both umbrellas. Cat and Griz both grinned at Timothy. Rags waved to Kenneth. Malvina went to the bar and ordered four Fantas. The quiet conversations of the Swedes and Germans were drowned.

Even the noise made by the girls was overwhelmed by the next clap of thunder, which sounded not more than a yard above the bar. It was the loudest, longest and nearest thunder Timothy had ever heard; he was frightened. He glanced at the girls. Rags and Griz were frightened by the thunder. Kenneth was also frightened, but he hardly showed it because of his training.

The rain thundered on to the roof of the bar with a new ferocity. The black and teeming world outside was torn by flashes of lightning so frequent and protracted that it seemed white more often than black. The thunder was almost continuous too; some came from far away over the plains, but much was directly overhead.

Euan came into the bar. He had an umbrella in one hand, a flashlight in the other, and his bundle of typescript under his arm. The typescript looked saturated, but Euan himself was dry, elegant and unperturbed. He smiled at his daughters, his fiancée, his future stepson, and his employee. Timothy realised that Cat's smile was her father's smile.

Euan said, in moments allowed him by the thunder, 'What an interesting storm. A cyclone immediately above an anticyclone, and the centre of both is here. Of course the lightning is striking the high ground to the east.'

'A few wildebeest are gonna get barbecued,' said Malvina.

'It is possible. If so Dieter will, perhaps, get it on film. A bolt striking a densely-packed herd—macabre, but unusual.'

'Dieter out there *filming*?'

'Yes indeed, with Renate.'

'Oh man.'

'Filming and recording. Even on the high ground they should be safe. Their car is insulated from the ground by its tyres. Of course, if they have not returned by first light, Cat shall go out to look for them.'

'Sure,' said Cat.

'A violent electrical storm,' said Euan to Timothy, 'figures among my ideas for our story.' He tapped the sodden bundle which he still held under his arm.

Soon it was dinner time. Timothy did not think it was dinner time but the Crombie girls did. They splashed across to the dining hut under their umbrellas. Timothy got partly under Euan's umbrella; his steps were guided by Euan's flashlight. The hard-packed dirt of the path between the buildings had become very slippery. It was still raining and the lightning was as vivid and the thunder as appalling as ever.

The appetites of the Crombie girls had not been affected by the storm, nor by the change of environment. The food, as Renate said, was excellent. Course followed course. The soup gave the girls a renewed opportunity to show how quickly they could eat soup. Kenneth was allowed to eat his soup and a little stew. His mother ate a few dry biscuits; she had sufficiently nourished herself with gin and tonic. The table was lit by candles. The effect was pleasing, even romantic. The candlelight gleamed on Cat's spectacles; Timothy wondered what she looked like without them. Plates, glasses and cutlery were of a higher standard than in Euan's house. Water was drunk. The rain thundered on the roof as loudly as on that of the bar. It was cold.

It was remarkable that Kenneth was so little influenced by the girls. He had been living with them in Euan's bungalow for some weeks, in a position to observe them closely at every meal. Visibly they enjoyed their food and their unorthodox method of eating it. He had made no attempt to modify his table manners in imitation of theirs. Indeed the reverse had perhaps taken place: to strict English training had been added a negative reaction, resulting in a fastidious style of eating that was almost incredible, almost odious, in one so young.

Mrs Morgan-Evans never drank coffee. The girls did not want coffee. Kenneth was not allowed coffee. They all embarked, with umbrellas and flashlights, on the journey back to their bandas.

Euan and Timothy had coffee. The rain was as hard as ever but the thunder had moved a little way away. This enabled Euan to speak, which during the meal he had not attempted owing to the noise of the thunder and of his daughters. He began at last to tell Timothy about the script. He tried to refer to the typescript, which he had placed under his chair, but it was of no use to him. It was sodden and illegible; it was a bundle not of typescript but of compost. Euan shrugged and smiled at Timothy.

He said, 'Dieter and I have many miles of film almost all of which is unique. If it were not unique we should not have troubled to get it. A few weeks ago, for example, not far from here, we filmed for six consecutive hours the copulation of two leopards. A great deal of this material has never been seen. It remains to be used.'

'I see,' said Timothy. He helped himself to more coffee. The coffee was excellent. Brandy would have gone nicely with it.

Euan said, 'When I was a lad, at school in Perthshire—a private school similar in character, I judge, to that which young Kenneth has been attending, and after which the Eton even of those days was a paradise of permissive tolerance—when I was a terrorised nine-year-old, we used to be set an exercise in English. Our instructor was a Mr Cleghorn, a man of wrath. It was Mr Cleghorn's whim to inscribe in chalk on the blackboard a number of unrelated words, as it might be 'violin', 'sulphur', 'Matterhorn', 'democracy', 'purple'. Our task was to construct a story in which these words were to find a place. I found it, even then, an exercise of the grossest futility. Now I might wish to write a story about the Matterhorn. I doubt it, but I might. If I did, the words I chose to communicate my vision of the Matterhorn could derive only from that vision; to introduce sulphur or democracy would call only on the mechanical ingenuity of the solver of jigsaw puzzles, a quality which is neither useful nor admirable. You understand me, Timothy?'

'No,' said Timothy.

'Oh dear. I thought I was explaining so well. I mean that our story must not be contorted to accommodate, because it exists, the footage that we have. I shall not play Cleghorn, cane in hand, to your youthful Crombie.'

'Oh I see. But if the story should lead, if we can make it lead, to copulating leopards—'

'You have perfectly taken my point. I made sure you would.'

'We don't want to drag them in. But you don't want to waste them.'

'I do *not* want to waste them. The footage in total represents a very large investment. The investment is mine. It includes no sponsorship, co-production, or finance of any kind. It includes Dieter's not inconsiderable salary, as well as the heavy expenses of safari. It is highly desirable that I should recoup the outlay, especially as I am getting married. Behold me Cleghorn, my dear Timothy, not with a cane in my hand but with an appealing look in my eye.

I am Cleghorn become a Landseer spaniel. I do not dictate. I suggest only. I even beg. However, the story that I have in mind does, I think, offer you the elasticity, the absorbency, the omnivorousness which will enable you, without outrage to your artistic conscience, to—'

'Write in a scene for copulating leopards?'

'Just so.'

'What is the story?'

'It is a saga of survival. I told you that my thinking began with your piece in the magazine, with the notion of a vehicle destroyed by an elephant whose feelings, and proboscis, had been hurt.'

'Yes.'

'Into our vehicle go not your somewhat fustian characters, but two very different persons. They are a father and daughter. The father is killed by the elephant while saving his daughter's life. The daughter is thus entirely alone in the African bush. She faces hunger, thirst, storm.'

'Storm. Yes.'

'This very storm, as well as others which we have filmed and recorded at various times. She travels, all alone, amongst predators of all kinds.'

'Leopards.'

'Leopards mercifully preoccupied.'

'That does work.'

'Yes, it does, doesn't it?'

'Who is cast as the girl?'

'Ah. Have you noticed the cyclic quality of the entertainment business? It is, in that regard, like meteorology, though faster, much faster. There was an epoch of the child star, of Shirley Temple and Freddie Bartholomew. Then for forty years there were almost no children in pictures, the few who appeared being, in most cases, repellent. This was itself a cyclic phenomenon, a return to the era of Baby Leroy. *The Lord of the Flies* might be regarded as Baby Leroy writ large. No, on second thoughts it could *not* be so regarded. Be that as it may, we are now embarked, most evidently, on a new child star epoch. Witness *Paper Moon.* A picture with a television spin-off. Which is, I need hardly tell you, a producer's dream. Theatre distribution covers the outlay, then you make the real bread. I confidently expect a television spin-off with our picture.'

'The daughter is a child? A little girl?'

'It is my daughter Morag.'

'Morag?' asked Timothy blankly.

'She will use, professionally, the abbreviation of her name by which we know her at home. The American market will jib at Morag. As a matter of fact her mother jibbed at it. She would have preferred, for all our daughters, names like Greta, Norma, Myrna and Loretta. But the names they have are traditional in my family. As my brother has had only sons, it fell to me to use the old Scottish names for my daughters. My mother, who holds passionately strong views on almost all subjects, would have been very distressed if Grizelda had been Greta. It is a topic my mother will almost certainly discuss, if she joins us here, which I half expect her to do. I agree with my mother; at the same time one mustn't forget South Bend.'

'South Bend?'

'Indiana. The heartland. "Morag" there would suggest the surname of a television cop, not the Christian name of a Scottish waif. She will be Rags. Rags Crombie, in ... I'm sure we shall arrive at a zap-zap commercial title.'

'I'm a bit confused,' said Timothy. 'The father is killed at the very beginning?'

'Right at the head of the picture. Before the main titles.'

'Then the child is entirely alone?'

'Utterly.'

'So there is no dialogue?'

'None. Are you very disappointed?'

'No.'

'She can soliloquise a little. Children do. She can address animals and birds. Again, children do.'

'Does Morag?'

'Certainly. She talks incessantly to her snake, when at home, and here to the McDavitts' mongoose.'

Timothy nodded. It was true. He said, 'Who will play the father?'

'An extra,' said Euan. 'The cheapest available. Requiring no transport here and expecting no pay. In a word, myself. I do not require lines to be written for me. I require that *no* lines are written for me.'

'Right.'

'You appreciate the merit of the opening? It relieves us of the expensive necessity of a featured player, a member of Equity. It gives us a valid reason for the child's abandonment in the midst of the wilderness. And it gives us a crapping great grabber start with enough action to knock your balls off.'

Timothy agreed that the opening, as planned, had many advantages.

Euan rose and elegantly stretched. His mane of hair was like a halo in the candlelight. The eyes of all the Germans and all the Swedes turned to him and stayed on him. Timothy had not much noticed their arrival, but they had all arrived and were demurely eating. Bill looked up from his soup and waved to Euan. Mollie looked up but did not wave.

'Goodnight, Timothy,' said Euan. He smiled Cat's broad, sweet smile. He picked up his umbrella and flashlight and strode out of the door and away.

Timothy had another cup of coffee. It was cold. He thought about the film. He thought it was a good idea, a commercial idea. He thought Disney must have made something very like it, but Euan must have been into that. And of course they could, legitimately, use all the wonderful footage Euan had, the leopards and storms and marvels.

Timothy stood up and went to the door of the building. He was stiff after his fall and after sitting for so long. All the Germans and Swedes had returned their attention to their plates. None looked at Timothy. Neither Bill nor Mollie looked at him. It was still raining, if less hard then only a little less hard. The thunder still crackled, but a long way away and at long intervals. It was dark, insanely dark. Black rain teemed in the blackness. He needed an umbrella and a flashlight. He had neither. Nobody had told him to bring an umbrella or a flashlight from England. He should have been warned. Somebody should come to him now, with light and comfort, to help him to his bed and keep him dry. He was suddenly terribly tired.

He stepped out into the pouring rain and turned in the direction he thought correct.

CHAPTER 7

Dieter and Renate found Timothy some hours later. He had been sitting, hugging his knees, at the foot of a tree, for a long time. The rain had stopped but everything was very wet. It was cold. The night was intensely dark. Animals screamed and jabbered in the forest, not very near but not very far away either. Timothy felt not fright but simply a total despair. He had been swallowed by primitive nature as soon as he had left the dining hut. He had walked a few paces and then fallen, slipping on treacherous wet mud. Struggling on through the rain, he had lost sight of the lights of the building. He lost them and all other lights, irretrievably. He saw no more lights, found no buildings or cleared spaces, found only a tangled and saturated wilderness. After quite a short time he realised he must wait for the dawn. But he was illuminated, instead, by the lights of the Bruckners' Land Rover. They revealed that he was beside the track, twenty yards from where the other cars were parked and from the office.

Dieter stopped his Land Rover and Renate got out of it. She helped Timothy to his feet. She did not ask why he spent the night sitting under a tree by the track. He did not explain. They gave him coffee from a thermos; it was warm. Renate led him to his banda. She had a flashlight but it was suddenly unnecessary: the sky began to lighten as they made the journey to Timothy's banda. The tropical dawn came as quickly as the tropical dark. Renate remarked on the wetness of the ground. Timothy assented, speaking without difficulty. She said that they had had a useful night, getting what Dieter thought would be excellent footage of the lightning. Timothy expressed gratification. They spoke softly so as not to wake up the people in the other bandas.

The first things Timothy saw in his own banda, into which dawn was rushing, were a big flashlight and a rolled umbrella. He dried himself and went to bed.

Screams and jabbering, like those of the night, woke him from troubled dreams. The voices were not those of fanged beasts, but of Euan's two youngest children. They were conducting an argument, stationed at opposite corners of Timothy's banda and out of sight of each other; this caused them to shout more loudly than usual. They were agreed that, during the night, they had both heard a leopard killing a baboon; they differed about the age of the baboon. Grizelda said that, from the noise, it was a very young baboon; Morag said that a very young baboon would not have been off by itself away from the troop. They agreed, secondly, that a buffalo had gone through the clearing, behind the huts, but they differed about the size of the buffalo.

'Somebody loused up the tracks,' said Grizelda.

'You loused them up, tramping all over them.'

'These my prints, stupid?'

They crashed round Timothy's banda, as had the buffalo, joining to examine the tracks.

'Geez, who went for a walk in the middle of the night?' said Grizelda.

'Maybe it was early in the night.'

'No, it was after the rain stopped. Look at these footprints. Rain didn't fall on these footprints.'

'That's right. The rain stopped around two thirty.'

'The guy took a walk after two thirty.'

'Pretty lucky he didn't meet the buff.'

'Pretty lucky he didn't meet the leopard.'

'These are Tim's footprints.'

'Horsefeathers.'

'They are too. His and Renate's.'

'Bull.'

'They are too. Lookit. Bata boots, new soles. Who has new Bata boots around here? Yah. And these are sneakers. These are the sneakers Renate wears. Wow, Tim and Renate, how about that?'

'They only met each other yesterday.'

'That's what they pretended, I guess. We don't *know* they only met each other yesterday.'

'That's right, we don't, do we?'

'Maybe they knew each other for years.'

'Suckered Dieter all this time.'

'That's why Tim *came* here.'

'Suckered Euan and came out here.'

'Tracks go right into the banda.'

'Wow. These British.'

'Euan's just as bad.'

'Euan's worse.'

'I'm hungry.'

'I want eggs.'

'I want cereal, four scrambled eggs—'

'Fried for me. Fried and turned.'

'Sausages, bacon, ham, toast.'

'Marmalade. The marmalade here is pretty good.'

'It's exactly the same marmalade they have everyplace else.'

'In California? In Detroit? In London?'

'Everyplace else in *Kenya,* dummy.'

'You didn't *say* that. Yah. You said everyplace else. You didn't say anything *about* Kenya.'

They went away.

Timothy found that he also was hungry. He thought with pleasure of scrambled eggs, sausages, bacon, perhaps not ham also; he thought of toast and Kenya marmalade and a great deal of coffee. This reverie, though brief, was enough to suggest that he was undamaged by the way he had spent the night. He was short of sleep, but he was not trembling with tropical fever. He was in any case immunised against malaria by pills, against yellow fever and typhoid and cholera by injections, and against smallpox by revaccination. He doubted if spending part of a night in the rain would, under the least favourable circumstances, lead to smallpox; but it was nice to know that he had averted the small risk.

It was also a comfort to remember that Euan was an expert on tropical medicine.

Timothy rose and washed. He observed that it was a beautiful day. The sun was getting high over the sullen yellow river. The time was 8.30. While shaving, in water that was slightly warm, Timothy re-opened the cut on his chin. He used some of Cat's words but not as loudly as she used them.

Dressing, he found that his remaining tropical clothes were wet and muddy. The clothes that had gone into the river had not yet been returned by the boy scout, and these other clothes were all wet. This was not surprising, not at all, nothing could have been more confidently predicted. But it was gravely embarrassing. Timothy found that he was underequipped. He should have bought, and brought, many more of everything. He had not expected rain and mud, but at worst, sand that could be shaken out of things. He had not been warned. People could have warned him, a lot of people, but none had done so. What, meanwhile, was he to do? He wanted his breakfast very badly indeed. But he recoiled from putting on his wet and muddy clothes. They would quite spoil his enjoyment of the scrambled eggs. At last he put on tennis shorts, elderly and amply cut, his pyjama jacket, a sweater, and bedroom slippers. The pyjama jacket was not altogether hidden and not at all camouflaged by the sweater. His top half was too hot and his bottom half too cold. For a moment Timothy lost courage: he could not and would not expose himself to a mocking world, in brilliant morning sun, in these absurd garments. But hunger drove him out of his banda towards scrambled eggs. The paths were still wet mud; his bedroom slippers were at once in a mess. Alicia had given him the slippers, which were made of a kind of tapestry. Timothy reflected that he was a writer, entitled to eccentricity. Anyone who thought his clothes were funny could crapping well think so.

A lot of people were having breakfast, out of doors, at large tables. Food was being cooked by a black in a chef's hat; he had great sizzling pans on a gridiron over an open fire. The smell from the pans was wonderful.

Timothy approached bashfully. Glancing down at himself, he thought his clothes were ridiculous but his pink-and-white knees were more ridiculous still. A good deal of Malvina's Mercurochrome was visible: a ragged vermilion map, resembling Spain, on his left leg, and a smaller map, perhaps Crete or Rhodes, on his right.

At one of the tables sat Euan, Cat, Malvina, Mrs Morgan-Evans, Kenneth and Mollie McDavitt. At another sat Grizelda, Morag, Dieter, Renate and Bill McDavitt. The remaining tables harboured Swedes and Germans. Euan was thinking. Cat and Malvina were eating bacon and eggs. Mrs Morgan-Evans was drinking tea; her eyebrows went up as she drank, as though she could scarcely believe the evidence of her taste-buds. Kenneth was eating toast with delicate refinement. Mollie McDavitt was looking at Mrs Morgan-Evans with an expression of open hatred.

Bill waved at Timothy, Renate smiled at him and Dieter winked.

Kenneth Morgan-Evans said, 'Good morning, sir.'

Cat did not look up from her eggs and bacon.

Bill said, 'Go and commission what you want, old boy. Old Peter there in the big titfer will fry you up a fry-up in a brace of shakes. Like a banger? Tea or coffee? Come and take a pew, plenty of room.'

Timothy ordered his breakfast. He sat down surrounded

by goodwill. No one remarked on his clothes; they were not, to be sure, any odder than those of the Germans or Swedes. Neither Dieter nor Renate referred to the events of the night; neither Grizelda nor Morag referred to the footprints in the mud.

Timothy liked this place and these people. He did not like them all but he liked most of them. The scene was, with qualifications, delightful. The sun was warm but not yet very hot. It had not dried the trees or the ground, but kindled an infinity of drops. If there were a good many flies there were also quite a lot of birds. Breakfast was not at all bad.

Euan came up. He smiled his enchanting smile. He said, 'This is, I think, a morning for reconnaissance. I want you to see the locations of our first four sequences. Forgive me, I put that badly. I suggest that it may help you to see the locations which we suggest for our first four sequences. You agree? Oh good, how kind of you. Dieter? Renate? Can you two spare the time? Oh good, good. But on no account hurry your breakfast, any of you. Let good digestion wait on appetite, and our locations on both. *À bientôt.*'

An hour later Cat drove them away from the Lodge in her father's Land Rover. Much of the grease, but not all, had been removed from her arms. She was subdued. She did not give Timothy the smile to which he had become accustomed. The track from the Lodge was muddy and treacherous after the heavy rain. Cat changed into the lower range of gears and drove carefully through the mud. The Land Rover skidded and slithered but it did not get stuck.

They drove to the place of the young cow elephant. The little herd was no longer there. Cat stopped the Land Rover.

'The car,' said Euan, 'will go along this path. We pick it up first with an aerial shot which establishes the terrain. The shot tightens and goes with the car.'

'What car?' asked Renate.

'Any car. An expendable car.'

'This heap is pretty expendable,' said Cat.

'It is a possibility. It has done an enormous milage, and I bought it second-hand from a safari company. And of course I could claim the insurance.'

'What?' said Dieter. He looked shocked.

'Without *suggestio falsi,* and only a little *suppressio veri.* The demolition of an elderly Land Rover. What do you think, Timothy?'

Timothy pondered for a moment. He tried to visualise the car and the elephant. The picture which came into his mind was that which had illustrated his story: but it was the wrong sort of elephant. He said, 'I think it would be more effective with an ordinary car. A smallish ordinary saloon, quite new and shiny.'

'Why? Forgive my peremptory querying of what may be, what doubtless is, a position to which you have arrived after due creative thought.'

'A Land Rover belongs here. You expect to see it near elephants. It's part of the African landscape. But a small, bright-coloured, shiny Peugeot is exotic here. A Fiat. A Mini if you like. It's the trappings of Western civilisation in the bush. So it's more—shocking to see it destroyed by the elephant.'

'That is right,' said Dieter unexpectedly.

'Yes,' said Euan slowly. 'The concatenation *is* more shocking. The allegory is more pointed. Brute nature, in primal innocence, betrayed by gimcrack mechanism and wreaking primal vengeance. Fancifully put, but I hope you take my point?'

Timothy took the point, as it was the one he thought he had himself made.

'Pity,' said Cat.

Euan said, 'Father and daughter are driving along this track. No dialogue. Perhaps a smile exchanged. He pats her hand as he drives, or rumples her tousled head. Relationship is thus established. Then we cut away to a single bull elephant.' Euan turned from the front seat to Dieter in the back. 'We can use one of Tannenburg's bulls. He won't charge much, after the favours I've done him. Of course the bull needn't destroy an entire car, but only the shell of one. Ranjit Singh can find us a body that looks all right.'

'Yes. It need not be heavy. We shall air-freight it down to Tannenburg.'

'Ranjit Singh won't charge us much for a shell of a car.'

'He will maybe give us one,' said Dieter, 'if we give him a credit in the titles.'

'I think he will.'

'Ranjit Singh has a big garage in Nairobi,' Renate explained to Timothy. 'He always has many wrecked cars. There are many accidents on the roads in Kenya because the people are fatalists.'

'Also drunk,' said Dieter.

'Sometimes drunk also, especially on Saturday night. Ranjit Singh collects the pieces of the cars. We will match a wrecked car from Ranjit Singh with a nice new car which we will hire and quickly return.'

'But who is Tannenburg?'

'He is a man who has elephants in Botswana.'

'Mohammed,' said Euan, 'shall go to the mountain. The pun is intentional, though more obscure than I would have wished. We can spray Ranjit Singh's car to match the car we hire. Then we can match this location with part of Tannenburg's farm.'

Timothy absorbed, with dismay, these revelations about the way the film was to be made. He said, 'You cut backwards and forwards between characters here and an elephant destroying a phoney car on a farm in Botswana?'

'The alternative,' said Euan, 'is to fly all of us to Botswana for two weeks, and also there to secure a car to match Ranjit Singh's illusory remnant.'

'Our way,' said Dieter, 'I go to Tannenburg for maybe three days, with the piece of car from Ranjit Singh.'

'I maybe go too,' said Renate.

'I shall need to be convinced,' said Euan, 'that that is necessary. The best wild-life shots are taken by a man on his own with a hand-held camera.'

'I go for the trip,' said Renate. 'I pay the fare.'

'Ah, then all my objections disappear.'

Timothy's objections did not disappear. He said, 'But will the locations match?'

'Trust Dieter,' said Euan.

Dieter said, 'When I shoot here I make an exact record of the distance of the car from the edge of the forest, and of the height and angle of the sun.'

'But the kind of trees?'

'Some trees will be sharp focus *there*, because the elephant is under the trees. They will be soft focus *here* because they are background, far away. I will cheat the shots a little, tilt the camera, reverse cut.'

'All this we have many times done before,' said Renate.

'But,' said Timothy, 'the elephant kills the father.'

'Not on screen,' said Euan.

'No?'

'Good gracious, my dear fellow, this is family entertainment. Would you have an adored parent trampled and gored? When an angry bull elephant kills a man, you know, pieces of the man are apt to be somewhat widely dispersed. Let us give ourselves credit for a little ingenuity.'

'Oh. Yes.'

'Now—the car stops. Why? Because the father, keen-eyed, has observed that it is overheating. This is not the result of negligence on his part. He is not culpable. The car is new, and has a fault. He gets out and opens the hood. Steam pours from the radiator.'

'How do we make the car boil?' asked Timothy.

'Dry ice,' said Dieter.

'So,' said Renate. 'The supply plane shall fly it from Nairobi. We shall order it by the radio telephone.'

'The father,' said Euan, 'will decide to allow the car to cool before refilling the radiator and proceeding.'

'As in *Wife & Mother*,' said Timothy.

'Is it so? Surely not. Father and daughter withdraw to the edge of the forest, to the shade. They use *that* route, and arrive at *that* spot. He takes, as they walk there, her little hand in his great paw. She trots trustingly beside him. No dialogue. Indeed, no live sound at all.'

'But the child talks,' said Timothy unhappily. 'You said she talks to animals and birds.'

'Dubbed,' said Euan. 'There is an excellent dubbing studio in Johannesburg. The vocal artiste will be my old friend Margot Champion. Though almost seventy she can sound more like a little girl than any little girl. She will love your script. She lives in Johannesburg. She will charge us very little.'

'Is very expensive,' said Renate, 'to have sound recordists and all equipment here. Is cheaper to dub.'

'Is better,' said Dieter. 'We have beautiful wild track, a big library of tapes. We have all animals, thunder, wind, birds, rivers, aircraft and cars, everything.'

'Yes,' said Timothy. 'But how and why is the father killed? If we don't see it, how do we know it's happened?'

Euan turned to look at him. He smiled Cat's smile. 'As to that, we are in your hands.'

'Oh I see.'

'The solution of such problems is the reason for your presence. You know elephant. You know men. You know the situation. You know the precise location. And you know that I do not want to fly the whole crew to Botswana.'

'The whole crew?' said Timothy. 'Is this the whole crew?'

'Yes. We leave union rules a long way behind when we come here.'

'But—'

'Your experience accustoms you to regiments with clapper-boards, with reflectors, with megaphones, with no function at all related to actual filming, to the extravagant idiocies of large studios, to make-work and featherbedding and a vast, needless payroll. What do we need to get footage into the can? Producer and director, myself. Lighting cameraman and camera operator, Dieter. His assistant, Renate. If sound recording is required—and more wild track is always acceptable—they are sound recordists. Continuity girl, Renate again. The cast is with us, not expensive. The props surround us. Wardrobe? Make-up? No problems. Transport? Cat is our driver. All the locations are within a few miles of the Lodge, which is why we chose it. Catering? The hospitable McDavitts. Laboratory, editor and dubbing mixer await us in Johannesburg. We shoot sixteen mil and blow up to thirty-five. For television we take a dupe neg of the sixteen. Have I left anything out? If a sense of fitness requires you to require a tea-boy, you shall be he.'

'Oh,' said Timothy. 'I didn't know you could make a film like that.'

'Nobody else can,' said Euan. 'But my last fifty-five-minute television special sold in twenty-eight countries.'

CHAPTER 8

After lunch Timothy sat on the bank of the river outside his banda. He sat, in his ample old-fashioned tennis shorts, in a camp chair from the banda; on his lap was a pad of lined copy-paper and in his hand a ballpoint pen. The sky had clouded over but the clouds did not immediately threaten rain. It was warm. Timothy had taken off his sweater, revealing the whole of his pyjama jacket. If people didn't like it they could lump it. His second lot of wet and muddy clothes had been taken away by the boy scout who had charge of him; Timothy hoped that they, and the first and muddier lot, would shortly reappear, or dinner would pose problems not solved as easily as those of breakfast and lunch.

At the foot of its banks the Rigu river swirled, yellow and menacing. The crocodiles and hippos were still hiding below its opaque surface. The top of the far bank was densely wooded. No buffalo or big cats were visible, but a troop of baboons was active in the big trees a hundred yards upstream. Timothy thought they were unseemly animals, owing to the mauve nudity of their behinds, but they were amusing to watch as they ran along the branches and slid noisily to the ground. At the edges of the river, and in the air between its banks, gaudy birds were catching insects. Butterflies larger than the smaller birds, brilliantly yellow and blue, flapped to and fro without obvious purpose. At the top of a dead tree a vulture settled; it folded its wings slowly, like two umbrellas. Timothy made notes of all these phenomena, for future if not immediate use. He was pleased with the observation that a vulture's half-folded wings resembled umbrellas.

He set to serious work.

His first need was for a title. He found it easier, writing anything, to start with a title. It not only set the mood, it also made the job real. A book or script with a title already had a kind of existence, before any of it existed. It became an active project, something in work. It conceptualised, separated, identified.

After thought, interrupted by the cries of birds and of Euan's daughters, Timothy wrote THE BABE IN THE WOOD in capitals on the first sheet of his pad. He was not serious about this title; it was not a title but a working title, something his time and Euan's money could be costed against.

Then he wrote, in proper form:

1. EXT. PLAIN AND FOREST. DAY 1.

AERIAL SHOT of wide expanse of African plain and riverine forest.

TIGHTEN to establish track at edge of forest. A small modern car goes slowly along track.

CUT TO

2. EXT. TRACK (MOVING CAR SHOT). DAY 2.

FATHER AND DAUGHTER. He driving, she beside him. Tropical clothes.

He touches her hand. She smiles at him. He rumples her hair, continuing to hold steering wheel with other hand.

CUT TO

3. EXT. FOREST. DAY 3.

Edge of forest, identical in character to (2) above.

A BULL ELEPHANT.

SFX: CAR ENGINE.

ELEPHANT reacts, raises head, flaps ears.

It was pretty easy so far. Timothy was writing in longhand but he could have been writing straight on to the typewriter, if his typewriter still worked. He continued in longhand. He cut back to the car, to a close-up of the temperature-gauge to the father's face reacting to the temperature-gauge, to the daughter's face, alarmed but trusting, to the front of the car and whisps of emergent steam. To the elephant, showing signs of interest, restlessness. To the car, a medium shot. The car stops. Steam visible. Father gets out, opens hood. Steam pours. Father shakes head, shrugs. Father grins ruefully at daughter. Daughter scrambles out of car. She puts grubby hand in his. Camera tracks with them to edge of forest. Father finds daughter place to sit down in shade. She sits. He sits. Her hand is in his. Cut to elephant, now on move. Cut to close two-shot of father and daughter. Reactions: alarm, dismay. Cut to car, elephant. Elephant explores innards of car with trunk. Cut to close-up of engine, trunk. Steam still visible, establishing car still hot. Trunk recoils. Sound effect: elephant trumpets with rage, pain. Cut back to medium shot: elephant, trumpeting, attacks car. Intercut reaction shots of father, daughter (Scenes 15 and 17).

So far a piece of cake. Timothy's problems now began.

After much thought he decided that the daughter s point of view was the trick. He would write it 'P of V', and it made the sequence work. She would be hiding, crouched on the ground under a bush. The father's death would be shot from her apparent P of V, which would be glimpses of the elephant seen through foliage. Dieter could muck about with his focus, and he could stick branches of anything he liked in front of his lens.

So: The child screams (in Kenya). The elephant hears, reacts (in Botswana). The child reacts, screams again (in Kenya). The elephant lumbers into movement, starts to charge (in Botswana). Father thrusts daughter into dense undergrowth, sallies out to divert elephant (in Kenya). Elephant now in full charge (in Botswana). Father continues heroic effort to divert elephant from child's hiding place (in Kenya). Child crouches in undergrowth, watches with horror (in Kenya). Reverse cut to child's P of V (actually in Botswana): elephant visible, father invisible (never, in fact, having left Kenya) owing to foliage, closeness of child's eye to ground. Father heard, shouting at elephant (in dubbing studio in Johannesburg). Elephant charges point where father presumed to be (in Botswana). Child's appalled reaction (in Kenya). Elephant, having disposed of enemy, goes away (in Botswana). Child emerges from undergrowth (in Kenya), finds father. Father dead but not mutilated. Cutaway to hyena, jackal, vultures aware of new carrion (in library). Tears of child. Dawning courage, resolution. Prayer for father. Child covers body of father with leaves, sets out on lonely, amazing journey.

Very good indeed.

Timothy wrote:

19. EXT. FOREST. DAY 19.

Tight CU DAUGHTER's face.

She SCREAMS.

CUT TO

20. EXT. PLAIN NEAR FOREST. DAY 20.

'Great Scott, old boy, what an industrious bloke you are.

Example to us all. Set fire to the paper if you write at that speed.'

Bill McDavitt stood grinning at Timothy. Binoculars were slung round his neck and he carried a stick. He said he was going on a bird walk. But he stood and talked to Timothy instead. He talked about bee-eaters, shrikes and trogons. Timothy was not nearly as interested as he pretended to be, but he did not want to snub Bill McDavitt. In his anxiety not to snub Bill he overplayed his enthusiasm for the conversation about birds. He gave the impression that nothing afforded him more exquisite delight than talking to Bill about birds. Bill, deceived, was thus unhappy about ending the conversation, although he would much rather have gone off and looked at the birds he was talking about. He did not say so but Timothy realised it.

Timothy at last said, 'Well, I suppose I'd better get back to work or my boss will be after my blood.'

Not many minutes later Bill proceeded on his walk. Timothy wrote about the elephant's reaction, in Botswana, to the child's scream.

'I would have thought they could have given you a desk.'

Mrs Morgan-Evans stood frowning at Timothy. She wore gumboots and a floppy hat. Her hair was coiled round her head. She looked like a librarian off to pick blackberries. Her nose twitched.

She said, 'They know perfectly well why you're here. They say they welcome you but they do nothing practical to help. Their welcome is all talk. That is not true hospitality as I understand it. My Gareth and I used to make a special effort. It was our pride to do so. Nothing was too much trouble. If a writer came to the Clock Hotel there would be a full inkwell in his room, blotting paper, and a printed card with the telephone number of the typewriting agency in Shaftesbury. "All the comforts of home and none of the bother." That was what we said about the Clock. No dogs, of course. Our cuisine was famous. My Gareth always said, good plain food doesn't have to be plain but it does have to be good. Menus in French and English. Our public rooms were a picture of elegance. The television room was very popular. We stood out against it for a time. We preferred the dying art of conversation. But in the end my Gareth said we were there to give our guests what they wanted, not what we thought they ought to have. Once the set was installed I became quite fond of it myself. I often used to view for a time, when my duties allowed. But I had to keep a close eye on everything. The chambermaids were all sluts. Emptying ashtrays into the toilets. Here, I suppose, they just fling their rubbish into the jungle. That is why there are so many flies. I shall not have a meal out of doors again, or allow Kim to do so. They can lay places for us indoors. That is what my Gareth and I would have done, without being asked. We would have sensed that a guest wanted special arrangements. Of course some guests were quite unreasonable. Americans. They wanted drinks brought up to their bedrooms. All the way upstairs from the bar. We allowed none of that sort of nonsense at the Clock. Simply giving trouble for its own sake. The McDavitts haven't the first idea how to run a place like this. I shall try to help them with a word in season. But I don't suppose I shall get any thanks. Far from it. Are you writing that nonsense of Euan's?'

'Yes.'

'Fancy putting Morag in a cinema film. I never heard of anything so ridiculous in my life. She has no talent. She is not pretty. She is almost retarded I sometimes think. They all are. Euan is absurdly indulgent. The mother is chiefly to blame. What can you expect of Americans? Drinks in their bedrooms indeed.'

She went away.

Timothy returned to the elephant. He covered another half page.

Malvina and Grizelda went by, along the path behind the huts, throwing a baseball at each other. Timothy waved to them. Grizelda waved back but Malvina ignored him. Timothy was mildly upset, but he was too preoccupied with his script to brood about Malvina's hostility. He completed the sequence. A tiny figure steps out along the track beside the forest. On one side of her stretch the illimitable plains. Her tears are dry but her lip trembles.

The sky began to darken. Timothy shivered. His boy scout appeared with clean and ironed clothes, scrubbed boots, and a hissing lamp. Timothy decided that he would dine at a proper hour, after a proper number of drinks: perhaps four.

Euan's family was assembled in the bar when Timothy got there. The German party had not yet appeared. The Swedes had left in a Minibus during the afternoon, but a French group had replaced them. The French had not reached the bar.

Kenneth said, 'Good evening, sir.'

Euan was thinking. Mrs Morgan-Evans was drinking gin and tonic. Neither reacted to Timothy's arrival. Grizelda and Morag greeted him with their usual enthusiasm. Cat said 'Hi,' but she did not smile her father's smile. Her face was without expression; she drank Tusker beer from the bottle. Malvina's face was not without expression: it was actively hostile. She said nothing to Timothy, but looked at him sullenly.

It began to rain just after Timothy reached the bar. There was no thunder. It was very dark. Timothy had brought his umbrella and flashlight. He put them where he could keep an eye on them while he asked the barman for whisky.

Dieter and Renate came into the bar, carrying flashlights

and umbrellas. Dieter winked at Timothy; he got whisky for himself and Renate.

The French group came into the bar, walking swiftly and close together, as though menaced but determined to make a fight of it. There were six of them, all about Timothy's age. They moved to the bar in a compact military formation. Their manner said that they were superior to their surroundings, but that they did not trust their surroundings to know it. The females of their species looked deadlier than the males, but the males looked pretty deadly too. They all spoke to the barman. They all spoke terribly correct English. They all wanted Scotch. Two of the men had moustaches. One of the women had a moustache, but in other ways she was chic and handsome. She was the dark one. The other women were fair. The fair women had faces made of expensive leather. They were formidable. They would shoot a lion as soon as look at it, and then skin it with their teeth.

Bill McDavitt came in; he fratted with the French. He found them as fascinating and delightful as all his other clients.

Grizelda and Morag began to clamour for food. The Crombies, the Morgan-Evanses and the Bruckners raised their umbrellas and surged towards the dining hut. Timothy was swept along with them. He was not able to dine at a proper hour, or drink more than one drink. He remembered his umbrella and flashlight.

Euan, the Bruckners and Timothy remained at the table drinking coffee after the others had left. Timothy said that he would type the first draft of the first sequence first thing in the morning. Euan said that he was amazed and delighted.

A senior boy scout brought a small exercise book to the table. In it, instructed by Dieter, Timothy wrote his name and the number of his banda; he wrote, 'Tea, 6.15.'

* * *

It was still pitch dark when the tray of tea appeared on the ground beside his bed. The air was cold and damp. A night-light flickered from a glass jar on the tea tray, warmly illuminating the tray but serving no other purpose. Timothy drank some tea. The mosquito-proof mesh over the windows of the banda paled as he drank. He pulled on all the clothes he could find. By the time he was dressed it was almost full daylight.

He began to type the screenplay, taking a single carbon, using two fingers, typing quickly but inaccurately because his fingers were cold. He worked in front of the banda, under the sky, in order to get the best of the light. The sun rose; it did not reach him owing to the forest by the river. The birds made a tremendous noise, but the typewriter made even more. It worked normally, but seemed to have become noisier. Timothy thought he must be waking the entire Lodge; indeed he was not averse to doing so; but no heads were thrust out of the other cabins, to marvel at his industry, as he hoped and expected. Some of the boy scouts, carrying boots and tea trays, came and watched him for a time. They were friendly, but they had to go about their duties.

At 8.20 Timothy had finished typing and checking his pages. The checking was extensive; it involved many unsightly corrections with his ballpoint, those on the top copy digging little trenches in the carbon copy. He put a paperclip on the top copy and carried it with him towards breakfast.

He passed Euan on the way. Euan was very elegant. His clothes were clean and beautifully ironed; no traces of sand or mud disfigured his boots; his chin and cheeks were shining with the precision of his shave; his mane of hair was tidy, almost glossy, and gave off a pleasing whiff of sandalwood; his eyes were as clear and bright as the morning sky; his smile was warmer than the early sunshine.

'Good gracious,' he said, taking the typescript from Timothy. 'Hoped for, but hardly expected.'

He began to read the script, standing on the mud path beneath a towering wild fig tree. He read the first page slowly and many times. Timothy saw that, as he expected, there would be nothing slapdash or superficial about his scrutiny of the script. Euan nodded to himself as he read; his face was inscrutable; there was no way of knowing whether the script was as good as he had hoped or as bad as he had feared. He took a tiny gold pencil from the pocket of his bush jacket; he made tiny notes in the margin of the typescript. After a long time he put the first page under the others and embarked on the second. A legion of birds clamorously occupied various levels of the wild fig tree above him; one of them dropped a substantial dropping, olive green, on his wrist. Euan noticed neither the impact nor the presence of the dropping.

Timothy waited anxiously. After all his years as a professional, the moment of submission, of appraisal, brought a small sick feeling to the pit of his stomach. It was his Latin prep shown up, when he was nine, to the Rev. James Catchpole; it was every script and story ever since. You searched for a response, while pretending not to; you waited, with dry mouth and thudding heart, for judgement.

Euan continued to nod gently and to make notes. He turned at last to page 3. Except for his nods and his notes he was motionless.

Timothy went quietly away.

They stood at the top of the path, the treacherous path, which led to the tethered boat in the treacherous river.

'I am infinitely pleased,' said Euan.

'Good,' said Timothy. He felt full of breakfast and joy.

'It is all more completely right than I dared expect.'

'Good.'

'We may regard these pages as a final draft.'

'Good.'

Euan smiled (Cat's smile, absent at breakfast, although she herself had been present). He stared down at the river and up at the tops of the trees.

He said, 'I wonder about the title.'

'Yes of course, that's not a serious—'

'Babe? Wood? It's a selling title. It may be right.'

'I'm not really putting it forward—'

'There is one other point. A very small one. But it is just worth bothering you with. As you know, screenplays have a double function. They are necessary for the making of films, whatever Andy Warhol may think. They are also of commercial value in themselves. They are marketable. Anticipating the film itself, they attract interest and finance, publicity, distribution deals. That bastard form the treatment used to be employed for these purposes, but the industry seems to have outgrown it. Even the crassest studio executive nowadays reads a screenplay, even a financier from Houston. This aspect should not be ignored.'

'Ah. Right.'

'You have made a decision, with which I concur, to open with a big aerial shot of the country. That presents no problem in a place where aircraft are almost as cheap to hire as cars. I think it would be a service to us all if the reader of the script, who has never seen what you and I have seen, is enabled, by a few words at this point, to see and to feel the awesome and savage magnificence of the plain, the lush and shadowy threat of the forest. Aridity and teeming moisture. Our child, our heroic waif, alone not in one primal environment but in two. Let us see and feel the two. Let us evoke the *genius loci*.'

'Right.'

'I hate to bother you with a revision.'

'Oh no, absolutely not, no bother.'

'Bless you for your forbearance.'

Euan stared with affection at the treetops and at the river and at the bird-thronged middle air.

He said, 'One other little point bothers me. You make, correctly in my view, the visual point that the car is new. This has two dramaturgic advantages. One is in the way of contrast, of shock. Desdemona must be blonde, palely beautiful, to be most horrifyingly throttled by the great black hands. Our little car must be spanking new to be most obscenely trampled by the elephant.'

'Yes.'

'There is, secondly, the matter of the boiling radiator. Why does it boil? Has the driver neglected to fill it up? Is he such a ninny? Has he placed his little one at risk by culpable negligence? No no, that is quite out of character. The car is new, just delivered, not yet run in. There are minor faults not yet revealed. One concerns the radiator. Perhaps the fan or fanbelt. Very likely the thermostat. We need not specify. We don't want to open that can of crapping beans.'

'No.'

'At the same time we must establish that the car is new, and that its faults are not the faults of our character.'

'I suppose so.'

'You sound unconvinced. Come, free and open discussion. I am always open to conviction. I am never more delighted than when offered a better idea than I have had myself.'

'Does it really matter why the car boils? Isn't the point of the opening sequence to grab the audience with the action, and at the same time to explain as quickly as possible why the child is all alone in the bush?'

'Perfectly put. It is nevertheless important, I truly believe it is mandatory, that the father should be the victim of ill fortune and not of his own incompetence. If he's the kind of man who forgets to fill his radiator, who cares if he's killed?'

'There is that.'

'A line or two of dialogue. Two or three lines. I shall not presume to try to write them for you.'

'Right.'

'No problem?'

'I don't think so.'

The shouts of Euan's daughters could be heard. They were conversing, but had not assembled.

Euan said, 'I hesitate to be dogmatic. You are the writer. But I think I should point out that to track with the characters as they walk from the car to the trees will not be easy. The ground, if you remember, is rough. Even if we had a dolly, and a lot of planks, I doubt if Dieter would manage a track. Do you feel it utterly imperative that the camera travels with the actors? May we not watch them start, cut to a panning shot as they pass camera, and pick them up when they get to the trees?'

'Of course. I should have thought of that.'

Euan smiled, as sweetly as ever before. He said, 'Yes you should. That was why we did the reconnaissance.'

Bill McDavitt went by at a distance. He waved. Timothy waved back. Euan did not see Bill. He was not in any case a natural waver.

Euan said, 'A final point.'

'Yes?'

'An aspect of, or rider to, the first. You and I know, and the Bruckners know, what artistes play these rôles. We can visualise them in the location. Some bluff fellow in Munich or Milwaukee will not know what Rags and I look like. He reads the script not knowing who the people are. Let there be a brief account of the appearance of each.'

'Right.'

'It's normal, I think?'

'Yes.'

'A minimal description, but such as may people the car with living, lovable characters.'

'I should have thought of that too.'

'Yes.'

'I'd better go and rewrite, then.'

'At your convenience. Just those few little points.'

'Yes.'

'Apart from which I repeat that I am enchanted with what we have.'

He handed the script to Timothy. He smiled.

Timothy walked slowly back to his banda. He felt tired. He sat down at his typewriter. He wrote:

1. EXT. PLAIN AND FOREST. DAY 1.

AERIAL SHOT of wide expanse of African plain and riverine forest. The plain is awesomely and savagely magnificent. The forest is lush, shadowy and threatening. The aridity of the plain contrasts with the teeming moisture of the forest. The SHOT establishes that there are two distinct primal environments here, not just one.

TIGHTEN to establish a track at the edge of the forest. A small, modern, shiny, spanking-new car goes slowly along the track.

CUT TO

2. EXT. TRACK (MOVING CAR SHOT). DAY 2.
FATHER and DAUGHTER. He driving, she beside him.

FATHER is tall, approaching middle age, tanned face, greying hair. He is neatly dressed in tropical clothes.

DAUGHTER is about 12, with long fair hair. She wears jeans and a T-shirt.

The next bit of the script would do as it stood, until

the father's reaction to the temperature gauge. Timothy wrote:

6. EXT. TRACK (MOVING CAR SHOT). DAY 6.

FATHER reacts to temperature gauge.

FATHER
(frowning
thoughtfully)
She's getting pretty hot.

DAUGHTER
(alarmed but
trusting)
But it's a new car! We only
got it today!

FATHER nods.

The next page stood. The tracking shot (for which Timothy blamed himself) was removed, and three cuts substituted. The remainder stood. And the whole crapping thing (said Timothy to himself) had to be retyped.

CHAPTER 9

Euan conferred with his fiancée outside her banda. Most of the conferring was done by Mrs Morgan-Evans. She talked quietly; Timothy, typing outside his own banda, could hear her voice but not what she said. Euan did more gesturing, and less talking, than was usual with him.

Timothy had not nearly finished his typing when Grizelda came to tell him it was time for lunch.

'Cat says you hafta go out in the Rover,' said Grizelda, 'so you hafta eat now.'

Timothy wanted a drink, perhaps three drinks, but he had lunch, at once, with the others. Mrs Morgan-Evans and her son were visible in the dining room, having lunch by themselves. Mrs Morgan-Evans had changed her clothes since the conference; she wore safari clothes and a big safari hat tied under her chin with a veil. Kenneth wore long grey flannel shorts, similar in cut to Timothy's tennis shorts, and a grey flannel shirt.

Mrs Morgan-Evans came with them in the Land Rover after lunch. She was still in a talking mood. She said, 'Euan tried to persuade me not to come. But since I am here I may as well try to take an intelligent interest in what he is doing. After all we are engaged to be married. That is something he seems to forget. My Gareth and I did everything together. He used to help me cast up the accounts, prepare the public rooms for wedding receptions, engage the servants, everything. It was a true partnership.'

'I am delighted that you should wish to join us, darling,' said Euan. 'I was only afraid that you would be bored.'

'I daresay I shall be bored,' said Mrs Morgan-Evans. 'But I have never shrunk from what I consider my duty.'

The Land Rover bumped down into a dry river bed and up the other side. Timothy was frightened. He thought the Land Rover was going to turn over.

Mrs Morgan-Evans said sharply, 'Look where you are going, Catriona.'

Cat made no reply. Her spectacles were very dirty.

They turned down a side track which joined the river. The bank opened into a broad hollow, scallop-shaped, full of trees and dense thorn bushes. The bushes were untidily festooned with dead vegetation, left behind by the river when it was in flood. They all got out of the Land Rover and went down into the hollow. Dense masses of red flies sat on the ground like pancakes; they rose, when disturbed, in noisy clouds, revealing the droppings of animals.

'Elephant,' said Dieter.

'Buffalo,' said Renate.

'Also buffalo.'

'The flies,' said Mrs Morgan-Evans, 'are almost as bad as at breakfast with those McDavitts.'

'It is here,' said Euan to Timothy, 'that Rags will shelter from the storm. She will huddle where Renate is standing, under the trees. It is lucky this place exists. We can pump water from the river, using power from a vehicle at the top of the bank.'

'At night?'

'We shall shoot night for night, yes. Dieter will have lights from a generator from the same vehicle.'

'What about elephant and buffalo?'

'What indeed? We may have an interesting night.'

'You're going to drag Morag here long after her bed-time,' said Mrs Morgan-Evans, 'and make her sit under a shower of water from that river? Her clothes and hair will be soaked. How will you get her hair dry before she goes to bed? Had you thought of that? Of course not. The whole idea is unthinkable. I wonder you even consider it. Mr Barnes must think of something else to put in your ridiculous film. Of course Morag is your responsibility, not mine, but you may remember that I am a woman and a mother myself.'

'Thank you, darling,' said Euan. 'An excellent point. We will arrange that a fire awaits us so that Rags can dry her hair.'

'That water is filthy,' said Mrs Morgan-Evans. 'Heaven knows what the child will catch if you pour it over her.'

'Maybe a catfish,' said Dieter. He winked at Timothy, who surprised himself by winking back.

Mrs Morgan-Evans continued to talk about the selfish irresponsibility of the project. She said that she had no intention of interfering, but that the scene must be changed. Mr Barnes must think of something else. Euan went into a trance. After a time Mrs Morgan-Evans shifted her ground. She said that Morag was incapable of sustaining the rôle of the child. She would not be able to learn what she had to do. She would not do as she was told. It was madness to expect an audience to sit through a whole cinema film of nothing but Morag all by herself.

Renate interrupted Mrs Morgan-Evans, which Timothy would not have cared to do. She said, 'But Rags will not be alone all the time, Phyllida. There are animals. Maybe Maasai. Different things with her, birds, snakes. And she will not be on the screen even one half of all the time.'

Mrs Morgan-Evans ignored Renate as totally as Euan was ignoring Mrs Morgan-Evans.

Dieter looked at Euan, then smiled at Timothy. He said softly, 'That is exactly how was his divorce.'

'Euan's?'

'Ulla is Swedish, but also American. I should say very American but that is maybe wrong. We have never been to America and must be careful about judging. You agree? Ulla went from Wisconsin to Los Angeles. She there met Euan. He was then a writer, but becoming a producer. Ulla has told me. They were quite happy for many years, but always she talked. This I have heard, Ulla's talk, it is endless. It is not unpleasant, you understand, but it never stops. So Euan grew shutters inside his ears. He learned to close the shutters when he wished. He could cut off all noise from outside, he could be alone with his brain. It was something we began to see, Renate and I, we saw the change on his face when he could hear nothing. You can see it now, yes? He can hear nothing. The shutters put Ulla into a rage.'

'So she talked more than ever,' suggested Timothy.

'Exact.'

Small lumps appeared in the smooth yellow water a little way downstream.

'Hippo,' said Dieter.

Mrs Morgan-Evans heard him. She turned to look at the lumps in the water. As though resentful of her inspection, some of the lumps reared up out of the water. A large part of a hippopotamus became visible. It was unimaginably ugly; it seemed to Timothy no smaller than an elephant. It opened an immense mouth, revealing two teeth like tombstones; it made a noise between roaring and hissing, very loud, at Mrs Morgan-Evans.

'It is a cow with a calf,' said Dieter. 'It will not attack now because there is much water in the river. They can submerge. When the river is low they are quite dangerous.'

Mrs Morgan-Evans turned away from the hippopotamus. She said, 'What a rude animal.'

'This,' said Euan, 'is professionalism indeed. What a joy it is to work with someone who delivers so rapidly, and who is not temperamental about suggestions.'

He and Timothy stood at the top of the bank above the boat. It was their place for script conferences. Euan handed the new typescript back to Timothy.

Euan said, 'I am more than happy with the few words

with which you evoke our locations. And with those that describe Rags. But ...'

Timothy waited. There would be more revisions, more retyping. A feeling of weariness afflicted him, like a weight on the back of his neck.

Euan said, 'I believe the father requires another word or two. You reveal him, to the reader of the script, only by saying he is tall, no longer a boy, and dressed for the climate. Remember, my dear Timothy, that this character, though minor in the totality of our drama, is about to die a hero's death. Let us see and feel him a *leetle* more clearly.'

Timothy nodded.

'As to the dialogue,' said Euan. 'In terms of mechanics it serves its purpose. It makes the primary plot points. But in terms of character? Are you, truly, satisfied yourself that character is established by these laconic and somewhat banal lines? *She's getting pretty hot. But it's a new car—we only got it today.*'

'I suppose it is a bit bald. But I thought the sooner we—'

'Speed is indeed of the essence. We don't want *Gone With The Wind* before the main titles. But are you, yourself, satisfied? Are you sure that these are the very best lines that can be given to characters whom we are meeting for the first time, one of whom is about to be killed and the other to occupy our attention for the next hundred minutes? The child may not need many more lines. Perhaps no more. The father, I submit to you, does. Something self-revealing yet understated. Something which, like all good dialogue, could be said by no other person, and said at no other time. *She's getting pretty hot.* Oh, Timothy. Is that what you came all this way to write? But of course I don't have to tell you what constitutes good dialogue. I merely,' Euan smiled, 'pay you to produce it.'

Timothy wrote:

2. EXT. TRACK (MOVING CAR SHOT). DAY 2.

FATHER and DAUGHTER. He driving, she beside him.

FATHER is tall and slim. Though muscular and athletic, his movements are graceful. His face is deeply tanned, but his complexion is clear and radiant with health. Though strikingly handsome, his face is that of an intellectual, perhaps an artist; though full of strength it is sensitive and perceptive. His keen grey eyes miss nothing. The hands that hold the steering wheel, with unmistakable skill, are, like the face, strong yet artistic, with the tapering fingers of a painter or musician. His clothes are expensive and elegant, but without the least vulgarity or ostentation; they are normal tropical clothes of cotton drill, distinguished only by their excellence of cut and material.

DAUGHTER is about 12, with long fair hair. She wears jeans and a T-shirt.

Timothy sighed deeply. He got up from his typewriter. He began to walk slowly towards the bar, past Euan's banda and that of Mrs Morgan-Evans. Voices came from the latter. Another catechism was in progress. Questions, in the sharp voice of Mrs Morgan-Evans, were answered by the demurer pipings of her son. It seemed that, surprisingly, Euan was also being taught algebra or Bible history: his pleasing tenor, subdued by classroom discipline, was to be heard answering, as though liturgically, a stream of questions from his fiancée. By creeping up to the side of the banda, Timothy could have overheard the lesson. It was a temptation which he resisted without difficulty. Malvina and Grizelda were in any case watching him, pausing from their game of baseball and from an argument about whether a duke was higher than an earl. Grizelda suggested consulting Timothy, who as a Britisher might know, but Malvina told her to shut up and play ball.

Timothy proceeded to the bar. He ordered, signed for, and slowly drank a large gin and tonic. The question of who paid for his drinks was still unanswered.

He went back towards his desk. The catechism was still in progress in the classroom. It seemed to Timothy that the questions were longer and the replies shorter and more muffled.

Timothy sat down at his typewriter, disturbing two bulbuls which were searching for crumbs among the keys. He wrote:

6. EXT. TRACK (MOVING CAR SHOT). DAY 6.

TIGHT CLOSE UP of FATHER's strong, intelligent, sensitive face as he reacts to the temperature gauge.

FATHER

(frowning
thoughtfully)
The temperature is more than
a trifle high. I suspect a grave
malfunction of fan or fanbelt.

DAUGHTER

(alarmed but
trusting)
But it's a new car! We only
got it today!

FATHER

(grave but
reassuring)

New cars, my darling, like
new creeds, often have
undetected faults.

That ought to hold him, thought Timothy. That ought to fix him.

He began to plan the storm sequence, the first night of the child's amazing Odyssey. He made an effort to remember the contours and features of the hollowed-out part of the river bank, where Rags would huddle from the deluge and from the crash and terror of electricity. It was an advantage that Timothy had himself had the experience of huddling from such a storm, lost and alone in the African wilderness. It was not at all often that he wrote with hard, recent, relevant experience; authenticity would surely breathe through every line of this part of the script.

The star herself came to tell him that he had to come eat, because he was to go out pretty soon in the Rover. Timothy went ate. On the way he passed Euan, who was standing in a trance on the path. He gave him the revised script. Euan took it, smiling Catriona's smile. Timothy went on to lunch, but Euan stood where he was, reading the script. Timothy ate out of doors with all the rest of them except Mrs Morgan-Evans and Kenneth, who ate indoors.

Catriona was not at the wheel of the Land Rover when they went out for their new recce. Renate said she was not feeling well. Mrs Morgan-Evans seemed to disbelieve this story, but did not declare out loud that Catriona was malingering, had lied to her father, or was insensible with drink or drugs. Dieter drove the Land Rover. Mrs Morgan-Evans again accompanied Euan, Dieter, Renate and Timothy; she was herself now accompanied by Kenneth.

He was dressed for a day at his boarding school in spring or autumn; he wore his grey flannel shorts, his grey flannel shirt buttoned to the wrists, a school or house tie, and grey woollen stockings with coloured tops. His shorts were held up by a belt in the same colours as tie and stocking-tops, mauve and yellow, an unpleasing combination, but one which Kenneth was evidently proud to have the right to wear. The belt was secured by a buckle in the form of a snake which had curled itself into the letter S; Timothy had had such a buckle to his school belt when he was himself eleven years old; he had not seen such a buckle for twenty years; it filled him with memories of his own dim but expensive private school, with memories of boredom, discomfort and fright.

It was not at once explained why Kenneth had joined the expedition. Euan seemed to have expected him, but his presence surprised Dieter and Renate. They exchanged a glance, which Timothy intercepted; Renate pulled down the corners of her mouth, a grimace which looked hard work owing to the stiff material of which her face was made.

Dieter drove for several miles. It was very hot and dusty. Mrs Morgan-Evans hated every minute of the drive, but only declared so by her sniffs. Kenneth's expression was unfathomable. He showed no interest in plain or forest, in the immense visible herds of wildebeest, the groups of topi, zebra and buffalo, the small herd of tall waterbuck in the shade at the edge of the forest, the troops of baboon, the circling vultures and eagles, of which there were disquieting numbers, or even the one elephant they saw. But when the film was discussed, desultorily, between Euan and Dieter and Timothy, he showed the keenest interest. His small blue eyes flickered from speaker to speaker. Sometimes his lips formed, noiselessly, the words someone had just used.

Euan said to Timothy that the script had moved from

the plane of competence to that of distinction. Timothy was a good deal surprised. He had intended the new dialogue as a joke. He thought at first that Euan was going along with the joke, straight-faced: but after a few minutes he understood that Euan was serious.

'New cars, like new creeds, have undetected faults,' he quoted sonorously.

He said that he was pretty satisfied, though not quite perfectly satisfied, with the description of the father.

'Here,' said Renate.

'So,' said Dieter.

He turned off the track and drove over the plain towards the river and its fringe of forest. He drove slowly, but the Land Rover bounced over the dry bumpy ground. The expressive breathing of Mrs Morgan-Evans became sibilant with outrage.

'Here,' said Renate.

'So,' said Dieter.

He stopped the Land Rover. The Bruckners looked at Euan.

Euan emerged from one of his briefer trances; he looked about him. He nodded and smiled, and thanked Dieter for driving them so well.

Euan said to Timothy, 'This is where we shot the leopards copulating.'

Mrs Morgan-Evans's intake of breath was like that of a person in terrible pain who is just, but only just, brave enough not to scream. She hit Euan in the back of the neck with her elbow; it was an ugly and even a foul blow, but was (as Timothy had to recognise) the nearest that she could come to a nudge when she was in the back seat of the Land Rover and he was in the front seat. As she dug Euan with her elbow she glanced meaningfully at Kenneth. Kenneth's eyes flickered between their faces; it was clear that he was following what was going on, but it was not clear what he felt about it.

'My dear Phyllida,' said Euan mildly, 'if Kenneth is unfamiliar with the word which describes the most normal and perhaps the most beautiful of all aspects of animal, as of human, behaviour, then it is surely time that—'

'Ssss!' said Phyllida, making a word with her intake of breath. The word expressed not pain but horror and contempt.

'Shall I select a different term?' asked Euan. His manner was pacific; he wanted the party to go smoothly; he wanted to get on with the job. 'Do you prefer, as I have noticed that my own daughters do, the inelegant but once acceptable Anglo-Saxon synonym? I am not certain that it is used in the Bible, but early seventeenth-century manners permitted the use of many words of similar character—of which, indeed, my daughters are also fond, and for which they could plead, if they wished, excellent historical precedent—'

'I will permit no discussion of the subject at all,' said Mrs Morgan-Evans.

'That makes a large difficulty,' said Renate, 'since it is a scene in the picture.'

'It must be removed. I will not consent to Kim being associated with anything of the sort. You seem to forget that he is only a child. I have tried to bring him up as a little English gentleman. What a good thing it is that I am here. Your film would not only have been ridiculous, but also pornographic.'

Dieter and Renate looked at her as though she were mad. Euan went into a trance. Kenneth intently followed everything that she said; his unblinking eyes were fixed on her face; his lips sometimes noiselessly echoed her.

Mrs Morgan-Evans continued to talk. She talked for a long time. She did not raise her voice. Her manner remained cool. Timothy tried to grow internal shutters like Euan's but their growth required more time. He heard everything that Mrs Morgan-Evans said. Most of what she said was dull but some of it gave Timothy a shock. She said, as though it were an agreed thing known to them all, that Kim as well as Morag would act in the film. There would be not one child lost in the wilderness but two.

'I cannot imagine,' said Mrs Morgan-Evans, 'why you did not have this idea yourselves. Its advantages are obvious. It will be far more interesting for the people who pay to go to see the film. Kim, fortunately, has a great deal of talent. He inherits that from my side of the family. I need hardly say that none of us was on the stage, but we were always outstanding in amateur dramatics. All of us. I used to get the most praise but I am not boasting about that. People used to talk a lot of nonsense about my going on to the stage or into cinema films, but of course I pooh-poohed such an idea. People said that I could have been a star. Very good judges said so. At school of course I was outstanding. It did not go to my head, I am glad to say. Kim happens to have inherited my talent. It will make everything far easier for Morag. She will not have to do so much. Indeed I think the less she does the better, don't you agree? It will be easier for Dieter as well. He will have Kim to photograph. You notice that his face is finely boned. It photographs extremely well. He gets that from me. My bone structure has always been admired. It is not a thing I brag about. Many artists have wanted to paint me, men of the highest reputation. I have been asked to sit by I do not know how many Royal Academicians. Of course I have always laughed at them. "The idea," I have always said.'

Kenneth's eyes never left his mother's face. His lips formed the words, 'The idea.'

Mrs Morgan-Evans twisted herself in the back of the Land Rover and addressed Timothy. She said, 'Of course the script will be quite different now that we have made this decision. It will be much better. You will be able to write conversations, which would otherwise have been impossible. I suppose writers like writing conversations? I know I would. Of course I have never had time to write. There are always more important things to do. I have always regarded conversation as an art. It is a dying art nowadays but a few of us try to keep it alive. Sometimes at the Clock Hotel it was a revelation to our guests. Many people said so. They went away enriched. You will also find that Kim will be good at learning his lines. He will work hard at it. I shall help him. You need not be afraid to write long speeches for him. I will see that he learns them off by heart. You may also have noticed that he has an excellent speaking voice. It is very clear and, of course, educated. It is a gentleman's voice. All my family have been remarkable for their diction. People frequently used to comment about it. A very distinguished man once said that he could listen to us by the hour. He said it was like the sound of distant church bells in frosty weather to hear us chatting. Sir Everard Snagge once compared my own voice to a boxwood flute. Of course I simply laughed at him.'

Kenneth's silent lips framed, 'Boxwood flute.'

Dieter turned the Land Rover round. The location was no longer relevant. He drove slowly back to the track and then more quickly back to the Lodge.

'Yes,' said Euan on the bank above the tethered boat. 'Ah, in a word, yes.'

'What is Kenneth to wear?'

'I believe Phyllida has in mind the garments he was sporting this afternoon.'

'His school clothes?'

'It is not as grotesque as your expression, a little pertly, suggests that you feel it to be. That neat, civilised school uniform, redolent of tidy classrooms and hygienic dormitories, dropped into these primordial wilds? It is not without effectiveness.'

Timothy wrote:

2. EXT. TRACK (MOVING CAR SHOT). DAY 2.

FATHER, DAUGHTER, BOY. FATHER driving, DAUGHTER beside him, BOY in back seat.

FATHER is tall and slim. Though muscular etc.

DAUGHTER is about 12, with long fair hair. She wears jeans and T-shirt.

BOY is about 11. He is neatly dressed in English school uniform.

FATHER touches DAUGHTER's hand. She smiles at him. He rumples her hair, continuing to hold steering wheel with other hand.

CUT TO

Timothy gave the revised script to Euan. He later saw Mrs Morgan-Evans reading it. Dieter was gloomy but Renate laughed.

CHAPTER 10

The weekly supply plane circled the camp, then landed on the airstrip two miles away. Bill McDavitt went to meet it in his Land Rover. The pilot came back with him, a young man with rimless spectacles and a studious face. There was a small amount of mail, mostly for Euan.

At dinner Euan said, 'I received today a delightful piece of news, which I had half expected. My mother is joining us here.'

The news provoked a mixed reaction.

Malvina said, 'Hot dog,' in a tone expressive of mild surprise rather than delight.

Morag said, 'Great,' without conviction.

Bill McDavitt said, 'My word, that is capital. There's nothing like a big family party, the more the merrier.'

Mollie said, 'I suppose she will want a chalet to herself. It will be very difficult to arrange. We really like at least a month's notice.'

Mrs Morgan-Evans said, 'While I am, of course, most anxious to meet your mother, a pleasure which you have not yet accorded me, I cannot help wondering if this is a sensible place for an old lady to venture to visit. Damp bedclothes, for example. And elderly people have to be very careful what they eat. Of course at the Clock we produced a special menu for our older guests. Our Senior Citizens, we called them. That was typical of the way we ran the Clock. Not everyone is prepared to take so much trouble. It is all a question of taking pride in what one does. I can't imagine what your mother will do all day. She will want to get back to Nairobi. Indeed I am sure she would be happier if she never left Nairobi. She could have a nice room at the New Stanley. You must book one first thing in the morning on the wireless telephone. We will see her when we return ourselves.'

Euan was not listening. This was evident from his face. He said, 'My mother will appreciate the birds here. She is quite an ornithologist.'

'Good show,' said Bill McDavitt.

'She may like to buy some paintings of birds,' said Mollie.

'I'm afraid,' said Mrs Morgan-Evans, 'that we shall all be too busy to look after her. It is an inconsiderate time for her to come. It would be much better if she postponed her visit. You must cable to tell her so.'

'My dear mother,' said Euan to Timothy, 'has a certain impetuosity. She tells me in her letter that she decided quite suddenly to come to see us all. It has happened before. She flew, she tells me, from Edinburgh, and with the minimum of delay and preparation flew on to Nairobi. She is now staying with the Basingstokes on Lake Naivasha. Lord Basingstoke is an ornithologist, which constitutes a bond. It is the only bond he has with any other living person. I do not think my mother will enjoy staying there long. I consequently expect her here in a day or two.'

'Top hole,' said Bill McDavitt. 'We'll have the welcome mat out and the ice in the jug.'

'We normally require a month's notice,' said Mollie.

It was a fine night. The sky was full of foreign stars. To take advantage of the weather, which might not be repeated, a fire had been lit under the stars in the open space near the bar. Immense logs were now burning there. A few canvas chairs had been placed round the fire by the boy scouts. Timothy accepted Dieter's invitation to join them for a nightcap by the fire. They sat down, but it was intolerably hot until they moved the canvas chairs much further back.

Renate said they knew Euan's mother quite well. She

had often been out to Kenya, though not to the Rigu.

Dieter said, 'It will be interesting to see her with Phyllida. With Ulla she was not successful. They were not happy together.'

Dieter said that he was tired. He shook hands with Timothy and went away to bed. Timothy offered Renate a drink and to his surprise she accepted. She asked him about his books. She said she would be interested to learn how he got his ideas. The truth was that, after he had run out of autobiography, he got his ideas from other books: but he told Renate that he relied on observation. He said that while she and Dieter observed and recorded the behaviour of animals, he observed and recorded the behaviour of people. Renate listened more respectfully to this rubbish than anyone in Timothy's experience. In most people this could only have been explained by stupidity, but in Renate's case Timothy thought it was to be explained by politeness. She was far too polite. She carried it to absurd lengths. But Timothy found it nice to sit near the fire under the stars and be treated as a celebrity.

Renate was so polite that she walked with Timothy back to his banda, still asking him about being a writer. It was during this walk, for which they both had their flashlights, that Timothy became aware of the leopard following them. It was clearly a leopard. The Crombie girls had heard a leopard near the Lodge. No one had contradicted them about this: they had not even contradicted each other. It could be accepted as fact that a leopard had been in the area. It had eaten a baboon. Timothy thought that he, even perhaps Renate, would be better eating than a baboon. It might be a lion following them. No one had recently recorded a lion at the Lodge, but they had often visited it. Dieter had seen, some months before, two young lionesses playing with a towel near the kitchen. Another person had found a lion in his banda when he went to bed; Bill McDavitt made a good story of his terror. Things like that happened all the time. It was taken for granted. It was part of life on the Rigu river. There was no comfort at all in thinking that the animal in the trees might be a lion rather than a leopard.

The lion or leopard moved very quietly, keeping pace with them, a few yards away from the path. Timothy stabbed the beam of his flashlight towards the small noises that it made, but the undergrowth was very thick and he could see nothing except foreign foliage.

Renate said, 'The path is not that way. The path is this way. See. Your rondeval is there.'

Timothy said, 'Yes,' in a high voice.

Renate said, 'A topic I find interesting is the matter of style. I do not know how to ask this question, but does a writer, a good writer, choose a style when he writes a certain thing? Does he say, today I will write in the manner of Goethe, because of what I am writing today, but tomorrow in the manner of Thomas Mann? Do you plan so? Please forgive me if the question is a stupid one but you see it is a topic which I find interesting.'

Renate had not heard the lion or leopard because of talking so much. Timothy did not mention it in case she thought him a coward. He knew he should offer to walk with her to her own banda, in order to fight off the lion or leopard when it attacked her. This would, however, involve his walking alone back from her banda to his. The prospect was too frightening to contemplate. The fact that she called her banda a rondeval, although it was square, made no difference at all. He did not want Renate to be killed by the lion or leopard, but if he had to choose he would choose her death rather than his own. Of course it would be hard on Dieter, who seemed quite fond of her. His own death would not be widely noticed but it might upset Alicia. It would also be unfair to Euan at this early stage of the screenplay.

Renate talked for a few more minutes by the door of

Timothy's banda. She spoke quietly so as not to wake the others. She said, 'If I were a writer I think it would be difficult for me not to copy other writers.'

Timothy, for whom copying other writers was a prerequisite for writing anything, agreed that plagiarism was a very real problem.

The lion or leopard had stopped when they did. It was still in the dense undergrowth beside the path, several yards from the banda. Probably it would not attack Renate.

After a time Renate said goodnight and walked sturdily away with her flashlight. The lion or leopard did not follow her, but moved stealthily off in another direction.

Timothy went into his banda and made sure that the door was properly closed. Part of him wished he had never come to Africa.

He did not begin working very early in the morning in case the lion or leopard was still about. He decided to do nothing until after breakfast, and until after he had another conference with Euan.

He walked to breakfast through beautiful early sunlight. The sunlight and the smell of breakfast reconciled him to Africa. He was eating sausages when all the Crombie girls arrived. He expected them to sit at the table where he was eating alone, but they went to a different table. They did not greet him, not even Grizelda and Morag. Malvina glared at him, but Catriona simply avoided his eye. This was presumed rather than certain, as her eyes were invisible behind the dirt on her glasses. Timothy was puzzled by this; at the same time it made breakfast more restful.

Mrs Morgan-Evans intercepted Timothy on his way back after breakfast. She was carrying his typescript. She was wearing spectacles unlike either Alicia's or Catriona's, but resembling those of the pilot of the supply plane.

She said, 'I have a number of comments, Mr Barnes. In the first place it is surely obvious that Kim should sit in the front seat of the motor and Morag in the back. That arrangement will of course eliminate the caress which the driver gives to the child beside him when he is supposed to be concentrating on his driving. That will be an improvement. It is quite wrong for you to suggest that the driver should take his hand from the wheel for such a purpose. My Gareth was an extremely good and careful driver and he would never have done such a thing. And of course an English boy does not have his hair rumpled. His hair will be nicely brushed and I expect it to remain so. It will be he, and not the driver, who notices that the car has become too hot. He will point this out. You will have to write new words for him to say. He will draw the driver's attention to the instrument and suggest, politely but firmly, that the car is stopped. When the driver has come to a halt, it will be Kim who jumps out of the car like the good scout he is. He will open the front and see the steam. He will tell the driver about the steam. You understand? There is no need for the others to say anything. He will say that they must give the car time to cool down. He will then take the girl's hand and lead her to a shady place where she can sit down. She will of course scream when she sees the elephant. He will not scream. He is too plucky to do such a thing. He is an English lad. It is of course he, and not the elderly man, who saves the girl's life by distracting the elephant. It is typical of him. It will establish his character for the people who go to see the film. The old man will be killed because he is trying to run away. It serves him right. Do you understand quite clearly what it is you must do? Here are the pages for you to do again. I should like to see them as soon as they are done. Euan will probably want to see a copy too. I hope you have brought enough carbon paper. Please be as quick as you can.'

Timothy wrote:

2. EXT. TRACK (MOVING CAR SHOT). DAY 2.

FATHER, BOY, DAUGHTER. FATHER driving, BOY beside him.

DAUGHTER in the back seat.

FATHER is tall and slim. Though muscular etc.

BOY is about 11. He is neatly dressed in school uniform. His hair is nicely brushed.

DAUGHTER is about 12. She wears jeans, T-shirt.

CUT TO

3. EXT. FOREST. DAY 3.

Edge of forest, identical in character to (2) above.

A BULL ELEPHANT.

SFX: CAR ENGINE.

ELEPHANT reacts, raises head, flaps ears.

CUT TO

4. EXT. TRACK (MOVING CAR SHOT). DAY 4.

FATHER, BOY, DAUGHTER, as (2) above.

CUT to CLOSE UP of temperature gauge. The needle is in the red danger segment.

CUT to BOY. He reacts to the temperature gauge.

BOY

(frowning
thoughtfully)

I say, sir, she's getting
pretty hot.

FATHER

(alarmed but
trusting)

But it's a new car! I only
got it today!

BOY

(grave but reassuring)

New cars often go a bit wrong, sir, like new creeds. Don't you think it might be better to stop?

As FATHER obediently puts on brakes,

CUT TO

5. EXT. FOREST. DAY 5.

BULL ELEPHANT, as (3) above, motionless but alert.

CUT TO

6. EXT. TRACK. DAY 6.

The car has stopped. The BOY jumps out, runs round to front of car, opens bonnet.

STEAM pours from the radiator.

BOY

(polite but firm)

Boiling pretty hard, sir. We'd better give her time to cool down.

FATHER nods in respectful agreement.

BOY helps DAUGHTER out of the car. He takes her hand and leads her towards the trees.

FATHER gets out of the car and follows.

The next phase had been complicated mechanically; Timothy thought it was still dramatically strong.

Daughter is sitting in the shade. Father sits nearby. Boy keeps watch like the good scout he is. Elephant on move. Close-ups of father, daughter. Reaction: alarm, dismay. Close-up of boy. Reaction: pluckiness. Cut to car, elephant. Elephant's exploration of car, shock, rage. Elephant assaults car. Intercut shots of father, daughter, both terrified, and boy, still plucky. Girl screams. Elephant reacts. Girl screams at elephant's reaction. Father also shouts in incoherent terror. Elephant charges. Boy thrusts girl into dense undergrowth, sallies out to divert elephant. Elephant now in full charge. Boy continues heroic effort to divert elephant from girl's hiding place. Father begins to sneak away. Elephant reacts to new movement, changes direction of charge. Elephant kills escaping father, though death not seen, in spite of renewed and unimaginably brave efforts of boy to divert him. Elephant goes away. Boy helps girl out of undergrowth. Father dead, somewhat mutilated as though in punishment for cowardice. Tears of girl. Boy does not cry. Girl comforted by boy. Prayers for father, for own safety. Boy and girl set out hand in hand on amazing journey.

'I do not object,' said Euan, 'to the boy jumping out of the car to open the bonnet—the driver should, however, have told him to do so—nor to him remarking, in these suitably artless terms, on the phenomenon of steam. You have, however, gone a little wrong in making the boy the one who notices the temperature gauge. We have there a little dramatic falseness, an uncertainty of touch which has only to be examined to be revealed. The driver notices the gauge and remarks on it. The boy or girl—it does not matter which—pipes up that the car is new. The driver comments that new cars, like new creeds ... just so. You must certainly restore to him an apophthegm which no juvenile would frame. These are small points. Where I feel that you have gone fundamentally, conceptually wrong is in the immediate death of the driver. Having been at some pains to establish this character, let us get some milage from him. Let us keep our little group together, under his leadership, for the first part of the Odyssey. He understands animal behaviour, he can navigate, he will repeatedly save the lives of his little charges. Then, perhaps, by the intervention of hippo or of snake, he is killed under yet more heroic circumstances than we originally devised for him. You understand the dramatic merit of this structure?'

'No,' said Timothy.

'But it is so obvious. Though pitchforked into the wilderness, the children are not alone. They are protected, guided, led by the hand, taught the techniques of survival. It is this that makes their survival credible. Their sudden defencelessness is the more unnerving, yes? Of course it is.'

Timothy had taken an extra carbon. Mrs Morgan-Evans approached him, holding it like a fan.

She said, 'It is an improvement, Mr Barnes. I am sure you must feel that yourself. It will be much more interesting like this, and people will find it easier to believe. But there is an important piece you must put in. It should go in right at the beginning, before you use all that space describing the driver of the car, who has after all a very small and unimportant part. I expect you have already guessed what I am going to say.'

'Yes,' said Timothy.

'You must put in a description of Kim. After all he is much the most important person in the film. People will read the script who do not know what Kim looks like. Perhaps Americans will read it. They will never have come in contact with a little English gentleman. You must put in a piece that explains what he looks like and what he has been brought up to be. That will explain why he behaves so pluckily, never thinking of self. It is the old question of service and leadership. They are the same thing, you know. The leader is the servant of his men. Foreigners do not know this. Very few of them have been to proper English boarding schools, so they cannot really be blamed. They have had no chance to learn. Kim is form captain, you know. I imagine you are not surprised. Soon he will be a prefect. They call it 'pre'. He will be moderate but firm. He will be extremely popular, though he will never court popularity. He would not stoop to do so. He will not stand for anything underhand or shabby. Bullies will get short shrift from him. You must do an extra copy of the script so that Kim can start practising.'

Timothy's nightcap, by the fire, with the Bruckners, became a routine immediately. One night established a custom. After dinner they expected him to come to the fireside to drink whisky, and he expected them to expect him. It was an interval of sanity and of peace. Their conversation was sometimes interesting.

Dieter said, 'I begin to understand about Mr Evans.'

'Mr Morgan-Evans,' said Renate. 'Gareth. What a strange name.'

'What happened to him?' asked Timothy.

'He fell under a train. He fell off a bridge over the railroad just as a train was coming along.'

'An accident?'

'No, of course not. There was a high fence on the bridge, a railing isn't it? For safety of persons on the bridge, naturally. He could not fall off by error.'

The lion or leopard was watching them by the fire. It did not come very close. It followed Timothy to his banda. He made part of the journey with Renate, but she turned aside to go to her own quarters; he made the rest of the journey alone. The lion or leopard was much closer, keeping pace with him in the undergrowth near the path. Timothy was seriously frightened. He wanted to run, but he thought this would excite both the lion and the leopard and goad them into attacking. He thought he would trip and fall down, breaking his flashlight and perhaps disabling himself. It was better to walk, briskly but casually. He tried to whistle blithely to deceive the beasts of the jungle, but his mouth was too dry. He blew, but no whistle came out. He locked the door of his hut with fingers that hardly functioned. The mosquito netting over the windows would not keep out a big cat determined to eat him, but the old timers insisted that no predator, except of course a snake, would come into the building with closed doors and nets over the windows.

But a snake might come in. Why would a snake not? Timothy searched his banda for snakes with flashlight and pressure lamp, until it occurred to him that the moving light might attract lion, leopard, hyena and baboon.

After breakfast he wrote:

2. EXT. TRACK (MOVING CAR SHOT). DAY 2.

BOY, FATHER, DAUGHTER. BOY beside FATHER, who is driving.

BOY is about eleven, a very good-looking English lad with a handsome, fine-boned face and clear, plucky eyes. He is very neatly dressed in the uniform of a first-class English boarding school. His hair is well cut and nicely brushed. In his manner to the others he gives subtle but unmistakable evidence of a spirit of service and leadership, which are the same thing. He looks every inch a future prefect, since his expression is moderate but firm, and shows that he would never stand for anything underhand or shabby.

FATHER is tall and slim. Though muscular etc.

DAUGHTER, 12, wears jeans, T-shirt.

CUT TO

'Gosh, sir,' said Kenneth Morgan-Evans, 'however do you know so much about me?'

CHAPTER 11

An unfamiliar light aircraft, with raffish yellow wings, buzzed the Lodge the following afternoon. Bill McDavitt went out to the airstrip in his Land Rover; he brought back Lady Crombie. She was small, with wiry white hair and apple cheeks. She wore shorts, resembling those to which Timothy had had brief recourse, ample and wrinkled; they were joined to her boots by short, stringy legs, skewbald in colour, with over-sized kneecaps. On her head was a Tam o' Shanter bonnet of faded tartan. Her hands, skewbald like her legs, emerged from the cuffs of a well worn bush jacket; if her kneecaps were like other people's hips, her knuckles were like other people's knees.

Bill McDavitt presented Timothy, who had come to the office in search of paperclips. He found no paperclips, but shook hands, instead, with Lady Crombie. She smiled Euan's smile, and looked at Timothy with Euan's bright grey eyes.

'Barnes?' she said. Her voice was like Euan's too: gentle, beautifully modulated, precise, not quite affected, rather high and light. 'From "bairn" perhaps. Auchtermoor would know, my eldest boy, quite a dab at derivations and so on. The dominies try to catch him out, but he's too clever for them. "Soople" as we say in Scotland. Ye'll nae faze Dugald Crombie of Auchtermoor. I'm delighted to find yet another fellow Scot here. Of course we go everywhere. Auchtermoor says the Scot is the true Wandering Jew. Wullie McDavitt here is typical of our proud race.'

'That's right,' said Bill. 'My folk came from Aberdeen or Glasgow I believe.'

'There was a Colonel Sir Hamish McDavitt of Minch,'

said Lady Crombie. 'He married one of the Stewarts of Blaith. Her mother was a connection of our own, on the distaff side. Minch's piper, going round the table after dinner, died one night of drink, I remember, while playing *Elphick's Farewell to Killiecraskie*. He fell across the lap of an American lady, using the word in its widest and most generous sense, where his death agonies lasted for quite three minutes. Her deportment was not dignified. All she had to do was sit still, but she didn't have the training. Minch had them both removed so that we could get on with the conversation. We were discussing the price of mutton, and everyone was keenly interested.'

'Never heard he was a relation,' said Bill. 'Couldn't claim that.'

'But you *should,*' said Lady Crombie. 'Get on to Lord Lyon. Make sure your arms are properly matriculated. You may have to difference them. I believe there are sixteen quarterings. Are you armigerous, Mr Bairn?'

'Grandad settled at Bulawayo,' said Bill. 'A bit of a wild lad from all I gather.'

'Auchtermoor was the place for wild doings,' said Lady Crombie, 'when the bit staggie was off frae the hill intil the burnside, and the chiels took their dram after the shooting. My husband's great-uncle once burned his factor alive on the fire in the great hall. Of course it was all in fun. The silly man had some cartridges in his sporran, which exploded. Nothing like that happens nowadays. The virtue has gone out of us.'

She signed the register *Catriona Crombie of Auchtermoor,* then lit a very small cigarette.

Mollie came into the office. She said, 'We really require a full month's notice. I'm not sure exactly where we can fit you in. Some Italians are coming this afternoon.'

'Are you a Scot yourself?'

'No.'

'I expect you'd like some tea,' said Bill.

'I would not. If you knew what it did to your gut you'd never touch it. I'll have a dram though. Mr Bairn? Wullie McDavitt? It's good to find yourself among friends. Come away, then, there's enough dust in my throat to mop up every drop in Dewar's distillery in the fair city of Perth.'

Lady Crombie was reunited with her granddaughters in the bar before dinner. The girls emerged from the darkness like uncouth creatures of the jungle, loping, pushing at each other, quarrelling in a language derived from English but so degraded as to be hardly intelligible. They fell silent when they saw their grandmother in the harsh light of the pressure lamp on the bar. She was still wearing her Tam o' Shanter, and was smoking perhaps her fiftieth tiny cigarette since arriving. Catriona and Malvina bent to kiss her; Grizelda was on a level; she bent, but not much, to kiss Morag. There was no apparent constraint between the old lady and the children; there was no contact either.

Euan appeared, having been out filming buffalo with Dieter. He and his mother made long speeches to each other of formal, even oriental, courtesy. He bought her a large whisky, which she drank neat, and which was, by Timothy's fuddled computation, her fourteenth.

The McDavitts appeared. More whisky was bought, both by and for Bill, both by and for Timothy, both by and for Lady Crombie. Bill tried to chat up his newest guest, according to his amiable rule, but his opportunities were few and brief.

Mollie turned over the pages of the book which she reserved for her blackest moods.

Dieter and Renate appeared. Their meeting with Lady Crombie was cordial; they bought her, and she them, glasses of whisky.

A party of Italians appeared, even more recent arrivals. They began taking photographs of each other with flashbulbs; they did this not in a merry but a grim spirit. They moved furniture to and fro in the bar for reasons of composition, which they explained to each other in quiet, tense voices. Mollie watched them with tragic fury, but Bill thought it was a grand party and the Italians fascinating and delightful.

Mrs Morgan-Evans appeared with Kenneth. Euan presented his fiancée to his mother.

Lady Crombie tilted her ancient head, swallowed her dram at a gulp, and said, 'Welsh, are you?'

'My Gareth was,' said Mrs Morgan-Evans. 'His family were long established people in Builth Wells.'

'Are there long established people in Builth Wells?'

'This is my son Kim.'

'How do you do, Lady Crombie?' said Kenneth. 'I hope you had a nice journey.'

'Kimball O'Hara,' said Lady Crombie. 'Hero of my youth. He and Rob Roy. And Davie Balfour, for all he was a Whig. Of course we always held to the old line. When the Prince raised his standard we were there. And when the flower of Scottish chivalry was cut down by Butcher Cumberland at Culloden, there were hot salt tears at Auchtermoor. They proscribed us, so we took to the heather and the whin. We poached red Campbell's deer and the bairns lived on blaeberries and goat's milk. Och, yon were the hard times. Welsh, did you say? I mind a Welshman once came to Perth races and tried to sell tips on the horses. "I'd duck you in the pond," said Auchtermoor, "but I'll no poison my friend's cattle." So we knocked him down and ran him over with the car.'

'Let's eat,' said Morag.

'At school they call him Ken,' said Mrs Morgan-Evans. 'That or Morgan-Evans. It is only I who call him Kim. It is a mother's fancy. Since my Gareth went ahead to the Summerlands, Kim is all I have. I am lucky to have such a son. Any mother would be proud of him. We support each other as we tread life's path together. Often we are more like chums than mother and son. Many people have remarked on it. At the same time I do not approve of being possessive. Nor of softness. When I see children who have not had proper discipline I grow quite indignant. We used sometimes to get family parties at the Clock. Not as residents. We did not allow children. But in the public rooms. Some of them were past belief, ill-mannered and over-indulged. The girls were the worst. They always are. Little madams, some of them. I gave one or two the sharp side of my tongue. So the ship ran smoothly on through calm waters and through storms.'

'Ye'll no get storms in Wales like the storms we get in the Hielands. Euan, dear, will you very sweetly get Mummy a little whisky? And some for Mr McBairn. You have given it up, dearest, I know. How your brother laughed when he heard. He likes his dram and he earns it. Of course he also likes claret, and Burgundy, and hock. He is a very fine judge of wine. People often think that we in the Highlands are uncivilised, but some of the finest palates in the world are to be found in north Perthshire. We are cultured in other ways too. In music, for example. My own father's piper won seventh prize at the Methven meeting in 1903. And one of the keepers played the fiddle for our dances. *Strip the Willow, The Dashing White Sergeant, Hamilton House*. How those grand old melodies stir the heartstrings. The Sassenachs know nothing of it, do they, Mr McBairn? I mind so well the night the ballroom floor collapsed at Lochwinniehead. We were dancing a foursome, to the pipes of course. Just at the end of the *Strathspey* there was a great creaking and splintering, and three sets of dancers disappeared from our sight. Twelve poor souls, one of them a third cousin of my own, a Miss Blair of Inchquhiddie. She was one of those who were killed outright.'

'I often thought of the Clock as a ship,' said Mrs

Morgan-Evans. Her voice took on a gently reminiscent tone. 'My Gareth's hand and mine were together on the tiller. We made the crew jump to it, I can tell you. Everything was shipshape and Bristol fashion. Every sail drawing. Land ahoy! And a keen eye on the galley. Our cuisine was the amazement and delight of connoisseurs. Our baked jam roll was compared to a poem by one of our guests, a Mr Stringham.'

Morag had been asking to have dinner, not loudly but insistently, for a long time, Grizelda for a shorter time, unheard by Lady Crombie or Mrs Morgan-Evans. Timothy saw Catriona murmur to Malvina. Malvina nodded; she took her younger sisters away to the dining room. Catriona herself remained. It was impossible to guess why; it was impossible to say what or whom she was looking at, as the reflection of the pressure lamps glared off her spectacles.

Euan was thinking. He was not listening to his mother or to his fiancée.

Dieter and Renate occasionally glanced at each other as they listened to the two soloists. Their faces were bland. They were drinking steadily, though not obtrusively, like Timothy himself.

Kenneth Morgan-Evans stood beside his mother. His hair and clothes were terribly tidy. He looked steadfastly at his mother when she spoke, but his eyes wandered opaquely about the bar when Lady Crombie made her whimsical alternations between over-correct Oxford English and broad, patriotic Doric.

'Altogether too much talk,' said Lady Crombie restlessly. 'Too much gas, as we used to say. Isn't it about time we had a bite to eat, Euan dear?'

Without altogether emerging from his trance, Euan moved to the edge of the darkness. He there bowed. His mother, with Tam o' Shanter atop and cigarette in mouth, stumped in her shorts from light to darkness. Mrs Morgan-Evans followed. She was talking as she went. Kenneth followed her. Euan disappeared in the train of them all.

Timothy, Dieter and Renate began to laugh at the same moment. Timothy had not realised that stolid Germans could laugh with such abandon; he had not realised that he himself could. The loudness and helplessness of their laughter had a good deal to do with whisky. They all sat down because they were rather drunk and because they were laughing so much.

Timothy looked at Catriona. Her shoulders were quivering. She took off her glasses. Tears were starting down her cheeks from her gentle, myopic blue eyes.

Perhaps because he was drunk, Timothy found this intolerable. It was entirely past bearing. He got up from his chair and went unsteadily across to Catriona. He kissed her.

He realised that she was crying not from grief but from laughter.

Timothy kissed Catriona on the temple, but his desire and intention was to kiss her on the lips. He tried to do this, but she thwarted him by turning her head away.

'I love you, Cat,' said Timothy.

'You're drunk.'

'Yes. But I love you.'

'You're having it off with Renate.'

'No.'

'You like Renate.'

'No.'

'What?' said Renate. 'How rude.'

'I like Renate very much,' said Timothy carefully, minding his manners, as he had been taught. 'But you are wrong to suggest that I love her, or am having it off with her, if that means what I think it means. You are in error.' Contact with Euan, and with whisky, influenced the manner of Timothy's speech. He said, 'You must distinguish between the respectful attention which I pay to a friend and professional colleague, and the passion which I feel for you.'

'Passion?' said Catriona in a small voice, unlike her usual voice, a voice like that of Morag when she first woke up after puzzling dreams. 'But we trailed you. They watched you. They told me.'

'A lion has been trailing me. A leopard also. I snap my fingers in their faces.'

'No. That was Griz and Rags trailing you. They trailed you every night. They told me about it. I was sore.'

'Why were you sore?'

'Because.'

Timothy was very angry, but only for one and a half seconds. He kissed Catriona. She twisted her head away, but not as far as before. His kiss landed perceptibly nearer her mouth.

Timothy said, 'Ask Renate. Ask Dieter.'

Catriona pulled away from him. She looked earnestly at his face. She put on her filthy spectacles, and pretended to be able to see better with them than without them.

She said, 'Have I been a jerk?'

She smiled suddenly, the broad sweet smile of her father and, more rarely, of her grandmother.

She said, 'I think you ought to eat.'

Timothy nodded. He was aware of a stupid, drunken, happy smile on his own face.

They went out into the warm darkness. Timothy stumbled. Catriona held him up with an arm round his waist. They kissed. Catriona gave Timothy her mouth, but it was evident that she had kissed very few people before. She did not at all know how it was done. Her lips were tentative and frightened. She did not open them. Timothy wanted to be masterful, but she was much stronger than he was and he had drunk too much whisky. They gave up after a bit and went in to dinner with the Bruckners. As they went from the darkness into the light,

Timothy saw, on Catriona's face, the miraculous family smile.

The Italians were taking photographs of each other when Timothy arrived for breakfast. He asked for sausages, bacon, scrambled eggs, fried bread, and coffee. He drank a pint of orange juice from a can while he waited for his breakfast to be cooked, at a table as far as possible from the Italians. One of the Italian women was beautiful from certain angles, but Timothy was more interested in his orange juice. He had no trace of hangover.

The Crombie girls arrived, talking quietly. They came and sat with Timothy. Malvina smiled at him. Catriona was cleaner than Timothy had ever seen her. She had brushed her hair. She ordered a breakfast identical to Timothy's, having examined his plate, but in double quantities. She adopted new methods for eating her breakfast, also modelled on Timothy. She found evident difficulty, but persevered.

Euan announced another recce. Catriona was to drive as usual. Euan, Dieter, Renate, Timothy, Mrs Morgan-Evans and Kenneth were to come.

When the Land Rover was about to leave the car park, Lady Crombie strode up. She carried a thumbstick, a pair of binoculars and a flask. She wore her Tam o' Shanter and her shorts. She said that she would come on the expedition. She was not one to stay at home twiddling her thumbs when adventurous doings were afoot. Mrs Morgan-Evans pointed out that there was no room in the Land Rover. An obvious solution would have been for Dieter to drive instead of Catriona. Timothy hoped that this would not occur to anybody.

Renate said, 'I have some washing to do, of my small things which I do not like to give to the boys. I will stay.'

Timothy could not picture Renate's small things, and

made no extended effort to do so. He made room for Lady Crombie on the back seat of the Land Rover.

It was a longer drive than usual. Timothy was wedged between Lady Crombie and Mrs Morgan-Evans, beyond whom Kenneth was perched on the corner of the seat. Lady Crombie had difficulty with her thumbstick in the confined space. One end struck Timothy on the side of the head and the other jabbed his foot.

Lady Crombie said, 'Any fool can be uncomfortable on safari. And dry. And we don't want that, eh, Mr McBairn? A dram about the middle of the morn is the best way to keep the cold out. I'm an old campaigner, you know. Och, it's grand to be out in the backlands, as Johnny Tweedsmuir used to say.'

'Or back in the outlands,' said Euan.

'Hoots toots, laddie, ye'll no faze the auld wife.'

'Oatlands,' said Mrs Morgan-Evans, 'was the residence of my maternal Uncle. Oatlands Lodge, Beaconsfield. The garden, though not large, was the most beautiful I have ever seen. Of course I love beauty. So does Kim. We both do. It has always been a characteristic of our family.'

'Family characteristics,' said Lady Crombie, jumping in with almost indecent speed. 'What's born in the blood is bred in the bone, they say. There's a subject I could be on about by the hour. Take our lot.'

While she took her lot, Mrs Morgan-Evans's resentful breathing could be heard above the speaker's voice and the labouring engine of the Land Rover. The breathing was directed against Lady Crombie, against Timothy since he was wedged against her, and against Catriona because she was driving.

In his lucid intervals Euan directed Catriona. After he relapsed into trance, Dieter redirected her. Her hair was honey blonde. It smelled of shampoo. It had not smelled of shampoo at breakfast, but of cigarette smoke, so she had washed it since.

They came at last to the place they sought, which seemed to Timothy identical to many other places they had visited. Its special virtue was that Dieter had there shot, one evening a year before, a small pack of hunting dogs pulling down a wildebeest. He could achieve the effect of identical evening light, in the identical place, filming the Boy, the Driver and the Daughter.

Timothy dutifully inspected the area so that he could set a scene there. It was not interesting. A full inspection took five minutes.

Lady Crombie went a little way away, with thumbstick, binoculars and flask. She began stalking small birds in stunted thorn trees.

Euan and Dieter discussed angles and light. Mrs Morgan-Evans stayed close to them and Kenneth close to her. She interrupted them frequently. Kenneth said nothing, but paid close attention. Mrs Morgan-Evans dug into her bag, which she was carrying as though for shopping in Beaconsfield, and pulled out a school cap. It was in the colours already familiar from Kenneth's tie, stocking-tops, and belt. She gave it to him. He put it on, exactly level over his ears. It was a clean cap, with a small shield on the front.

Timothy turned towards the Land Rover. Catriona was still sitting in the driving seat. As soon as he turned towards her she got out. She smiled at him shyly. At this moment Timothy realised that he was in truth in love with her. He had told her so the previous evening, but he was drunk at the time, and they had been brought together by laughter. Now he was not drunk, but felt it, owing to the effect of her smile.

He went over to her and they stood, a yard apart, by the Land Rover. Catriona's cheeks were pink.

Timothy did not know what to do. Nor, it was evident, did Catriona. There was very little they could do. It was the first moment they had been alone together since the moment in the dark between the bar and the dining room. They were not really alone now; they could see, and be seen by, all the other members of the party.

They smiled at each other. It was not nearly enough, but it was all that suggested itself.

There were many things that Timothy wanted to say to Catriona, and to ask her, since she was still a puzzle to him. But what he found himself saying was, 'How on earth did your father meet Mrs Morgan-Evans?'

'He stayed at the hotel.'

'Good God.'

'And they got in the sack.'

'Was that before or after my Gareth—?'

'After, I guess. I don't think Euan brought *that* on. So she got knocked up.'

'You don't mean that Kenneth—'

'Hell, no.'

'Did she have the baby?'

'They got rid of it. It cost Euan plenty.'

'How do you know all this, Cat?'

'Euan told Mal and me. So I guess it's true.'

'Yes, it must be true. I don't care.'

'Me neither.'

'Oh I do love you.'

'You do?'

'Yes.'

'Why? Why do you? I don't get it.'

'You're not supposed to get it. There isn't anything to get.'

'Okay, if you say so,' said Catriona dubiously. 'I admit there's a lot I don't know.'

'Don't try and learn too fast. Don't change too fast.'

'I have to *change*, Tim.'

'You washed your hair.'

'Mal said I should.'

'It looks lovely.'

'It does?'

'You look lovely. I love you.'

'I love you too. Would it be okay if you kissed me?'

'Is anybody looking?'

'What the hell does it matter? Why is it a big secret? Do you want it to be a secret? It can be, if you want.'

'No secret,' said Timothy. 'Not even a little one. Have you kissed many people, darling?'

'What did you call me?'

'Darling.'

'Darling. I can take a lot of that.'

'Darling. Darling Catriona. My darling Cat.'

Catriona sighed. 'I can take a lot of that. Have I what?'

'Kissed many people?'

'Not since high school, and then I was never any good at it. What should I do?'

'You might open your mouth a bit.'

'*Open* my *mouth*?'

'Yes.'

'Are you sure about this?'

'Couldn't we try it like that? If you don't like it you can tell me.'

'Okay. But I don't want to *talk*. Should I take my glasses off?'

Timothy nodded. He felt his heart thudding in his throat. He did not want to talk either. He kissed Catriona. He found that her mouth was open. It was a better kiss, and went on longer.

'It's a little *wet*,' said Catriona at last.

'I think it's worth it, don't you?'

'I guess it is,' she said seriously. 'Only it takes a little getting used to.'

'Let's try again.'

Catriona wiped her mouth on the sleeve of her shirt, a gesture reminiscent of the Cat of yesterday. Timothy kissed her.

She said, 'You know, Mal isn't going to approve of any of this.'

'Why not?'

'Hygiene. Mal says you don't use another person's glass.'

'You do if you love each other.'

'You do? Oh, great. Okay, then.'

They got back to the Lodge in time for a late lunch. Lady Crombie, over the porridge she had brought with her, asked Timothy for a copy of the script. Timothy glanced at Euan, who indicated with a gesture of his fork that his mother was to be accorded every facility for reading the screenplay.

'It's a braw wee scriptie, Mr McBairn,' said Lady Crombie, in the bar, a long time before dinner. 'And I've had a bit clash wi' Euan aboot it.' She drained her glass, waited for Timothy to refill it, and continued in her other, Oxford voice, 'I made a suggestion about the story with which Euan has agreed. It will strengthen it very much.'

CHAPTER 12

'But my dear Timothy,' said Euan at the top of the bank above the tethered boat, 'think. A fascinatingly assorted group, yet wholly credible. At each crisis, a contrast of reactions. Strength complements weakness, weakness strength. Think of the visual spectrum. Think of the empathetic range, which has become almost universal. The very elderly will be able to identify directly into the action, the very young, and all in between. That cannot be bad, commercially. And it all costs no more money.'

Timothy's breakfast, eaten with Cat and the girls, turned to mud in his stomach. The air over the river was full of birds; they made too much noise and the colours were vulgarly bright.

Euan said, 'Of course the new structure throws more onus on the man, the one whom we have called the Father. Let us continue so to call him, to remind us that he is guide and protector of them all. He will not, of course, now be killed, either at the beginning or later, but will lead his little band at last to safety. The principal burden of dialogue will fall on him. This will in many ways simplify your task.'

Timothy wrote:

2. EXT. TRACK (MOVING CAR SHOT). DAY 2.

BOY, FATHER, DAUGHTER, OLD LADY. BOY beside FATHER, who is driving.

DAUGHTER and OLD LADY in the back seat.

BOY is about eleven, a very good looking etc.

FATHER is tall and slim. Though muscular etc.

DAUGHTER, 12, wears jeans, T-shirt.

OLD LADY in Scotch bonnet, shorts.

CUT TO

'Och, you've missed the point entirely, Mr McBairn,' said Lady Crombie. 'You'll have to do it again.'

Timothy wrote:

2. EXT. TRACK (MOVING CAR SHOT). DAY 2.

LADY, BOY, FATHER, DAUGHTER. LADY beside FATHER, who is driving. BOY and DAUGHTER in back seat.

LADY is not young but extremely vigorous and active. Her brain is as sharp as her eye. All her movements are graceful. Her face, which is crowned with exquisite silver hair, gives clear evidence of her aristocratic ancestry in the strong yet delicate modelling of the features. Yet although this is a face to break a myriad hearts, it is also one to give commands and to face danger and privation with unflinching resolve and high courage: looking at it one is inescapably reminded of forbears who poached deer and lived on blaeberries and goat's milk after suffering the treachery of other clans. Clothes as well as physiognomy show the LADY's pure Scottish lineage, as she wears a Highland bonnet and kilt (Hunting Crombie tartan).

BOY is about 11, good looking etc.

FATHER is tall and slim. Though muscular etc.

DAUGHTER, 12, jeans/T-shirt.

CUT TO

3. EXT. FOREST. DAY 3.

Edge of forest. BULL ELEPHANT.

SFX: ENGINE. ELEPHANT reacts.

CUT TO

4. EXT. TRACK (MOVING CAR SHOT). DAY 4.

LADY, BOY, FATHER, DAUGHTER, as (2) above.

CUT to temperature gauge. Needle shows v. hot.

CUT to CU LADY. Reacts to previous.

LADY
(frowning
thoughtfully)
The wee motor's running
muckle warm.

FATHER
(alarmed but
trusting)
But it's a new car! You only
got it today!

LADY
(grave but
reassuring)
New cars are like new creeds,
laddie. There's mony a snaggie
in baith. Ye'd best stop.

As FATHER obediently puts on brakes,

CUT TO

5. EXT. FOREST. DAY 5.

As (3) above. ELEPHANT alert.

CUT TO

6. EXT. TRACK. DAY 6.

Car has stopped. LADY gets out, strides gracefully to front, opens it. STEAM pours from radiator.

LADY

Ay, boiling like the kettle on the auld wife's hob. She needs a whilie to cool doon.

FATHER nods in respectful agreement.

LADY helps BOY and DAUGHTER out of the car. She takes their hands and leads them towards the trees.

Now: Lady on watch, keen, alert. Others resting in shade. Elephant on move. Alarm, dismay. Courage and resource on Lady's face. Car and elephant. Screams. Lady does not scream. Elephant charges. Lady sallies out, diverts elephant. Agility remarkable. Elephant goes away. Lady helps others out of hiding place, comforts them, gives courage. Lady leads party on first stage of amazing journey.

Timothy and Catriona had nightcaps by the fire with the Bruckners. It was the new routine. The Bruckners accepted it without comment. They correctly assumed that Malvina would take the children off to bed, while Catriona sat with Timothy by the fire. Dieter winked at Timothy, but it was not a lubricious wink. It had no trace of the complicity to which, as witnesses of Timothy's declaration of passion, the Bruckners could have felt themselves entitled. They were too polite for complicity. Dieter's wink was a friendly wink.

Timothy and Catriona held hands in the near-darkness by the fire. Timothy had a whisky and soda. Catriona did not want a drink.

Catriona had had a shower before dinner. Timothy

heard Malvina urging her to do so; he heard Catriona's shower thundering on the concrete in her hut, while he was drying himself after his own shower. Picturing Catriona in her shower sent him almost mad.

For dinner Catriona wore unfamiliar clothes. It was not easy all at once to recognise her. She wore a skirt. Her legs, which Timothy saw for the first time, were very nice. They were not at all like her grandmother's in form, texture or colour. She told Timothy she had borrowed the skirt from Renate. It did not fit her; it was too wide and much too short. She was self-conscious about the amount of bare leg which the skirt showed when she sat down. She saw Timothy looking at her legs; she blushed.

It was pleasant by the fire. The Bruckners were both in a talkative mood. They reminisced about other visits to the Lodge. Timothy could see Catriona's long bare legs in the firelight. He put his hand on Catriona's nearer leg, just above the knee. She jumped. She looked at him nervously. The firelight winked on the lenses of her spectacles. With his other hand Timothy squeezed her hand, intending reassurance. Her hand returned the squeeze. Timothy was relieved. It was all right, after all, to have his hand on her leg.

Timothy felt as nervous and uncertain as Catriona.

The Bruckners said goodnight and went away. Though still not asserting complicity, they were sentimental about Timothy and Catriona. They found it gemütlich. In their manner of saying goodnight they gave the young people their blessing.

Constraint set in. Now that they were alone together, under romantic circumstances, the evening should take a new turn. This was painfully obvious. But the new turn was not obvious at all. Timothy felt a bit silly with his hand stretched across and grasping Catriona's leg. It was not getting anybody anywhere. But to move it might frighten Catriona. To take it away, meanwhile, would be to retreat even from the bridgehead that he had.

Timothy made conversation. He asked Catriona about her life in Los Angeles. She answered his questions in a small, breathless voice. She, too, knew that something else ought to happen, but she did not know what and she was nervous. She seemed grateful to sit and talk, postponing the unknown. She said she had graduated from high school three years before. Her grades were no good. She did not want to go to college, and was not pressed to do so. The others would go to college. They were smart. She herself was dumb. They lived with their mother in Westwood. Their stepfather was a dentist. He was okay. He was pretty good about the girls. He didn't have to pay any dough for them, because Euan did that. Her stepfather made a pass at Catriona once, but she slugged him. The same thing happened with Malvina. Mal wanted to do premed. She wanted to be a doctor. She, Cat, had the idea of being a mechanic, getting some kind of qualification as a mechanical engineer. She went to a few parties in L.A. They were lousy parties. She had friends but no boyfriends. She knew some boys but none of them was her boyfriend. She had had boyfriends in high school, but since she graduated she preferred cars. She owned a few cars, which she had built or rebuilt.

Timothy understood all this without being able to understand any of it. Life in Westwood did not come alive in Catriona's account.

Silence fell again. The fire was low but still powerfully hot. A mound of incandescent ash radiated fierce heat. Catriona's face and legs were dimly visible in the glow of the fire. Timothy saw that she had taken off her spectacles.

He moved his hand a very little, very gently, on her leg.

She began at once to ask him urgently about London. He was only a writer, right? That was all he did? No job? Where did he live? Did he go to parties? How did he eat, cook his own meals or what? Did he have girls? How many girls? No, never mind about the girls.

They were sitting in canvas chairs, each with narrow wooden arms. Two wooden arms divided Timothy from Catriona. Until they got up out of the chairs he had reached the virtual limit of any advances he could make to her. Accordingly he stood up suddenly, and offered her his hands. She took them and he drew her to her feet. This was not necessary but she went along with it. They were thus standing close together and face to face, Timothy put his arms round Catriona. She put hers round his neck. They kissed. Her mouth, when Timothy's met it, was open. He felt her breasts through her shirt and his.

Her face was frightened when she withdrew to look at him. He could barely see it, but he could see that it was frightened. He understood.

He said, 'There's no hurry. Don't hurry anything. We have all our lives.'

'Yeah, but I feel so *stupid*. At *my* age.'

'We'll come to it gradually. Step by step. And when you're ready ...'

'Step by step. I like the first step. I got used to it.' She wiped her mouth with the back of her hand. 'Did I learn the first step?'

'Yes.'

'Teach me some more.'

'Now?'

'Yes. Now.'

Her face, in the faint glow of the fire, was full of resolve. It was alarmed, but she was going to go through with the next step. She would learn or bust.

Timothy took her hand. He lit his flashlight and led her towards his banda.

A faint rustling could be heard in the undergrowth near the path. Catriona stopped. She pulled her hand away from Timothy's. She darted into the undergrowth.

There was a scream. Catriona emerged, holding Morag by a fistful of hair.

'Leggo, you big bully, you're *hurting*,' said Morag, 'Hey, did you lose your glasses?'

Catriona put her glasses on. She marched Morag away.

Timothy waited for her in his banda, not undressing, by the passionate light of a single candle.

He woke in the dawn, cold, in his camp chair, dressed, with numb legs and a crick in his neck. The candle had burned out. He went to bed.

Malvina and Grizelda came to see Timothy after breakfast. Malvina was holding a copy of the new typescript.

Malvina said, 'Look, what kind of a crazy lousy deal is *this*?'

'The movie is supposed to be about Rags,' said Grizelda.

'Do you two want to be in it?'

'Hell no. But Rags does.'

'She is in it. She's one quarter of the entire cast.'

'Bull. They pushed her out. All she does is scream. One scream, and that's gonna be drowned by the others.'

'It's no fair,' said Grizelda.

'*She* has to be the star,' said Malvina. 'Whose side are you on, anyway? What's Cat gonna think when she sees this?'

Timothy wrote:

2. EXT. TRACK (MOVING CAR SHOT). DAY 2.

DAUGHTER, LADY, BOY, FATHER. DAUGHTER beside FATHER, who is driving. LADY and BOY in back seat.

DAUGHTER is about twelve. She is bewitchingly pretty, with an irresistible charm somewhere between urchin and fairy princess. Long golden hair, delightfully unruly, crowns a small face with tip-tilted nose and wide grey eyes. We see at once that this is a small person with perceptiveness, courage and power of command far beyond her years. She wears blue-jeans and a casual shirt, which show that she is a normal well-adjusted American kid.

LADY is not young but extremely etc.

BOY is about eleven, a very good looking etc.

FATHER is tall and slim. Though muscular etc.

CUT TO

3. EXT. FOREST. DAY 3.

ELEPHANT etc.

CUT TO

4. EXT. TRACK (MOVING CAR SHOT). DAY 4.

Temperature etc.

DAUGHTER

(frowning thoughtfully)

It's running pretty hot, Dad. I guess you forgot to check the fanbelt.

FATHER

(alarmed but trusting)

But it's a new car! We only got it today!

DAUGHTER

(grave but reassuring)

New cars are kinda like new creeds, Dad. Plenty can go wrong until you iron out the bugs. I guess you should stop.

As FATHER obediently puts on the brakes,

CUT TO

5. EXT. etc. 5.

6. EXT. TRACK. DAY 6.

Car has stopped. DAUGHTER jumps out, dances lightly round to the front, opens hood with confident skill. Steam etc.

DAUGHTER

Approximately 640 Fahrenheit, I'd say. Needs 27 minutes to cool down.

FATHER nods in respectful agreement.

DAUGHTER helps LADY and BOY out of the car. She takes their hands and leads them towards the trees.

Now: Daughter diverts elephant when it charges at craven screams of all the others. Daughter's agility wraith-like, balletic. Her courage that of well-adjusted American kid. Elephant baffled, retires. Daughter helps others out of refuge, comforts them, infects with own high courage. Daughter leads others on first steps of amazing journey.

The reactions to this version were discouraging. Euan, with unusual directness, reminded Timothy who was paying him. Mrs Morgan-Evans found him by the office; she drove him backwards, talking, all the way to his banda, into which he bolted. Lady Crombie cornered him in the bar.

After dinner, holding Catriona's precious but sticky hand by the fire, Timothy told the Bruckners about the script.

Renate said, 'It is hard on your fingers, but you must do four screenplays.'

'I only use two fingers.'

'It is hard on those two,' said Dieter, 'but Renate must be right, isn't it?'

'But when you shoot it?'

'Another problem for another day.'

'Rags really wants to be an actress,' said Catriona, in the voice which had become so unassertive and gentle.

'I shoot it so,' said Dieter. 'The shots will favour Rags.'

Bill McDavitt left the Italians, one of whom was playing a guitar in the bar, and stood in an outdoorsy pose by the fire. He withdrew a few feet almost at once owing to the excessive heat.

He said, 'A round on the house, eh? Any takers? To drink the health of the lovebirds. May all their troubles be little ones.'

It seemed that Bill had noticed about Timothy and Catriona, or perhaps been told by Morag when she went to visit the McDavitts' mongoose. Mollie showed no signs of having noticed; she had not been in a noticing mood. It was not likely that Euan had noticed; his mind was elsewhere and his ears almost permanently shuttered. Neither his mother nor his fiancée seemed to have noticed; their minds were elsewhere too. If Kenneth had noticed he had kept quiet about it. Timothy was relieved about this. He supposed some sort of statement would have to be made, perhaps a formal representation to Euan, but it was better not to be in too much of a hurry about it. Much was still vague. Many questions were still unanswered. Timothy did not know if Catriona wanted to marry him, or expected to. He had not asked her to. In a general way it was his intention to ask her, but not yet, not for a long time yet.

'When are you two getting married?' asked Bill, when the boy scout had brought drinks for them all except Catriona.

'Very soon,' said Timothy. 'Almost at once.'

Catriona looked at him. Her face was full of amazement and terror. She smiled.

Neither leopard nor Morag, neither lion nor Grizelda,

trailed them to Timothy's banda after the others had gone to bed. Catriona did not stay long. She did not remove any of her clothes. But for the first time they kissed in a comfortable position. Catriona's breathing was rapid and shallow. She shivered in Timothy's arms. Timothy also had trouble with his breathing and his whole body trembled. He felt very passionate but he restrained himself.

Timothy pondered Renate's advice. He recoiled from the work involved, but he admitted the wisdom of her idea. He prepared four versions of the opening sequence. He took one carbon copy, for his files, of the versions starring Euan and Lady Crombie. He took two carbons of the version starring Kenneth, so that Mrs Morgan-Evans could help the star to practise. He took three of the version starring Morag, so that her sisters could scrutinise it. The quantity of typing was enormous. Catriona, though restless, understood.

'Celebrate?' said Euan to Bill McDavitt in the bar before dinner. 'Celebrate what? When the picture is shot we may allow ourselves a modest celebration. When it is cut and dubbed. When it is marketed, syndicated, shown, reviewed. When I recover my investment. Then, by all means, a celebration. Engagement? But I have engaged nobody. I intend to engage nobody. I want no professional actors. That is an artistic as well as a commercial decision.'

'My Gareth and I,' said Mrs Morgan-Evans, 'always used to celebrate the anniversary of our meeting, which took place under romantic circumstances at Pontypridd. We both used to say that it was like something out of a novel. Not that I ever read novels. My life is too full. I work like a beaver. I always have done so.'

'More beavers about nowadays than there used to be,' said Lady Crombie. 'Of course there was always the old Marquess of Aberdeen, but now half the men you see go about covered in hair. Face-fungus we used to call it. Of course a moustache is quite different. Soldiers always wore them. Some were far too large. I refer to the moustaches, not to the gallant soldiers. Auchtermoor always says that a man with a lot of hair on his face has something to hide.'

'Hide?' said Euan. 'I remember once being compelled to hide, for eleven days, from a gang of pimps, in the laundry basket of a brothel. A curious episode. It was in Marseille, near the old port. I was making a documentary about prostitution which could, in those days, be shown in Anglo-Saxon countries only in so mutilated a form as wholly to distort the facts. I did not permit Mrs Grundy to wield her Philistine scissors. In Germany and Japan it was shown uncut, and in the latter country won an award, a cupro-nickel sculpture of obscure purpose and equivocal design.'

'I love sculpture,' said Mrs Morgan-Evans. 'Art and other forms of beauty have always been my greatest joy.' She began to tell them about the Peter Pan statue in Kensington Gardens.

'Designs,' said Lady Crombie at the same time. 'I could tell you about a few of them. There was a man called Barnaby had designs on a niece of mine, a Miss Carmichael of Balfilth.' She dilated on the plans of this bounder.

Mrs Morgan-Evans began to speak more loudly so that the company should have the benefit of her views. This encouraged Lady Crombie also to raise her voice. Soon they were both shouting. Euan, who might have been expected to go into a trance, felt that his experiences in the laundry basket were too valuable not to relate. He explained that the laundry was left in the basket for eleven days because it was Christmas. He listed the garments among which he was hidden. In order that those present should hear about them, he too began to cry out, as though addressing the waves of the sea, or a great multitude of persons who were chattering among themselves. He intoned, at the top of his voice, a roster of basques and petticoats.

'I don't think they twigged,' said Bill McDavitt to Timothy. 'But *I'm* jolly glad anyway. Bags of cheer-ho.'

Lady Crombie's voice gave out first, owing to her great age. It suffered a diminuendo, slow at first and then rapid, until it was entirely drowned by the voices of Euan and Mrs Morgan-Jones. She withdrew from a contest which had become unequal. She drank a number of large neat whiskies in resentful silence.

Euan's voice grew higher and thinner. He was not shouting but singing. His song went from the timbre of cor anglais to that of oboe, and then to flute breathily played. At last only the flautist's breath remained: the flute fell silent: Euan's manner remained urbane and his hair tidy, but no sound came out of his mouth.

Mrs Morgan-Evans said, 'At the same time I do like a picture to be about something. We had exquisite paintings in the public rooms at the Clock. In pride of place there was a study of an elephant charging. *Rogue Elephant.* It was over the fire-surround in the principal lounge, where our guests could relax in easy chairs and exchange views on the topics of the day. My Gareth's favourite was called *Chinese Girl* or some such. I never cared for it. She had been using green make-up. I daresay she was no better than she ought to have been. I moved it to the television room. Speaking of pictures, I have been thinking about our cinema film. What it needs is glamour. Beauty. I expect I realised that because beauty is so important to me. It is the breath of life to me. So I have decided that I had better be in the film too. It is not something I want to do. I am not anxious to have my name in lights, although I expect to see it there. It is simply that you are all so keen on the film that I feel I must do my bit to make it a success.'

CHAPTER 13

'Will you be able to manage?' said Timothy quietly to Malvina at dinner. 'On your own? Look after the kids?'

'Sure.'

'What is wrong with Griz?'

'She has blackouts. It's a mild form of epilepsy.'

'Oh God. I'm very sorry.'

'We have to watch out for her. Euan doesn't know about it. Look, you don't have to worry about us. You worry about Cat. She's *your* worry.'

'Yes, I know. But I'm not worried about Cat at all. Cat's fine. She's marvellous.'

'Yeah? She's okay?'

'That's the understatement of the decade.'

'What a crappy way to talk.'

Timothy nodded. It *was* a crappy way to talk. Nevertheless Malvina had understood him. She smiled. She had Catriona's smile, her father's, her grandmother's. Timothy had not often seen it on her strong and grubby face. She was really very like Catriona, but her features were more pronounced. Perhaps she was handsomer. Timothy felt a rising, disloyal surge of interest in Malvina, the smart one, the future doctor. He glanced to his other side, to soft sweet Cat, who was trying to eat like a lady and making slow work of a sand-grouse. He felt such a wave of love that Malvina was relegated into an honourable but secondary rôle as sister-in-law, attendant lady, confidante, good pal.

At the same time it was a bit unnerving. What would happen when Grizelda grew up, with the fascination of her illness? Morag, with her startling blondeness and her acting ambitions? Both of them so attractive, so affectionate, so demonstratively fond of him?

He glanced again, therapeutically, at Catriona. His doubts disappeared, or nearly so. She was a girl with nice sisters, although it was true that their table manners were not very nice.

'Is this what they call necking?' asked Cat.

'What a horrible word. Yes, I suppose it is.'

'Like heavy petting?'

'Yes.'

'It gave me a pain in the gut.'

'Me too.'

Mrs Morgan-Evans had a sinister hold on Euan. She controlled him by a monstrous magic. Although he ignored her part of the time, he danced to her piping another part of the time. He danced in private but the results were lamentably public. THE THRONG IN THE WOOD was one of the results. If Euan dared not defy his fiancée, it would be madness for Timothy to attempt to do so.

He wrote:

2. EXT. TRACK (MOVING CAR SHOT). DAY 2.

YOUNG LADY, DAUGHTER, OLDER LADY, BOY, FATHER. YOUNG LADY beside FATHER, who is driving. DAUGHTER, OLDER LADY, BOY in back seat.

YOUNG LADY is one of those to whom nature has been prodigal in its blessings. In her are combined, to a rare degree, beauty of face and figure with high intelligence and varied talents. Though so young, she is visibly competent to run a complex commercial enterprise as though she were the captain of a great ship. She is deeply sensitive to beauty in all its forms. She has high courage and indomitable optimism; although she has evidently suffered more than most, a brave smile is her most characteristic expression. Her hair is exquisitely arranged. Her voice is sometimes like a distant church-bell, sometimes like a boxwood flute.

DAUGHTER is about 12. She is bewitchingly etc.

OLDER LADY is not young but extremely etc.

BOY is about 11, a very good looking etc.

FATHER is tall and slim. Though muscular etc.

CUT TO

3. EXT. FOREST. DAY 3.

ELEPHANT etc.

CUT TO

4. EXT. TRACK (MOVING CAR SHOT). DAY 4.

Temperature etc.

YOUNG LADY

(smiling
bravely)

The motor car is too hot. You can tell that from the instrument here. Do you see it? I reminded you to look at the fan, and told you where it is, but I am afraid you forgot.

FATHER

(alarmed but
trusting)

But it's a new car! You only bought it today!

YOUNG LADY

(smiling reassuringly)

New cars are like new chambermaids. They have to be watched very carefully. Now stop at once and let me see what the trouble is.

As FATHER obediently puts on the brakes,

CUT TO

5. EXT. etc. 5

6. EXT. TRACK. DAY 6.

Car has stopped. YOUNG LADY gets out and, gracefully as a swan, seems to float rather than to walk round to the front. With dainty fingers she opens the bonnet. Steam etc.

YOUNG LADY

Just as I thought. We must give it, like the tempers of naughty little children, time to cool.

FATHER nods in respectful agreement and awareness of his own negligence.

YOUNG LADY helps DAUGHTER, OLDER LADY and BOY out of the car. She takes their hands and begins to lead them towards the trees.

Young Lady now diverts elephant from others, who have attracted it by their screams, calls to it in voice like boxwood flute. Elephant, pacified by magic of voice, goes quietly away. Young Lady has long speech on subject of optimism, smiling at danger. Young Lady leads others on first phase of amazing journey.

Kenneth walked, with tidy steps, to Timothy's typewriter-table on the bank of the river. He squeaked in his English sandals. He took off his school cap. His hair was nicely brushed.

He said, 'I say, sir, could I bother you for a moment if it's not bothering you? I don't think you ought to put my mater in the front seat of the car, because the person there is the one that's got to notice that the car's getting too hot. A lady wouldn't notice a thing like that, sir, not in a million quadrillion years. She wouldn't know how to open the front, either, specially if it's a new car they've only just got. It's more of a boy's sort of thing to do, sir, isn't it, really? Isn't a boy more likely to notice a car is getting hot? And to open the front? Isn't it really more the sort of thing a boy would do, sir, more than a lady? Also, I don't see how a lady can take three people by the hand, sir. I mean, it says here that the young lady takes the old lady and the boy and the girl by the hand and leads them over to the trees. I don't see how she can very well do that, sir, if you don't mind my saying so, not unless she has three hands, sir.'

'Eight pages in three weeks,' said Euan. 'I do not, I trust, use goad or spur. I am a man for carrot rather than stick. I have never believed in harrying writers. But, but ...'

'But,' said Timothy, 'the concept has undergone substantial modification every other day.'

'You exaggerate. Are you, as my preceptors would long ago have put it, making excuses? Nothing, I assure you, is less likely to mollify me.'

'I'll get on with the next sequence,' said Timothy.

'The storm. Good. Can I hope for the next eight pages in rather less than three weeks?'

'Is it your wish that the Young Lady, the Daughter, the Older Lady, the Boy or the Father should be the principal character?'

'You must strike a balance. You are the writer. I await your suggestions with keen interest.'

Timothy wrote the storm sequence in five versions. In the version starring Mrs Morgan-Evans, and that starring Kenneth, the characters were lucky enough to stay dry owing to the denseness of the foliage under which they were sheltering; in the other versions they all got a good drenching.

Then he wrote the sequence involving the copulating leopards. He only did this in three versions, as Mrs Morgan-Evans found the subject nasty.

A small, bright Simca was driven into the car park. It was washed and polished by a band of boy scouts. Catriona carried out a mechanical inspection of the car; she covered her own arms and Renate's clothes with black grease.

Catriona drove the car slowly up and down the edge of the riverine forest. A tiny aircraft buzzed the car repeatedly. Dieter Bruckner sat beside the pilot, a camera bolted to the door.

Timothy went with Catriona. They could not be seen by the camera because of the car's roof. An open car would have been better for the film, but no small new open cars were available for hire. The closed car made problems for Dieter, but it was better for Catriona and Timothy. They could not really use the time, except to talk and be together, as Catriona had to drive the car up and down the track; but they talked and they were together. Catriona had not washed, nor changed out of Renate's grease-fouled little skirt. The muscles of her legs vibrated as she used the clutch and accelerator and brake of the car. There was a small amount of grease on her thighs and a smear of it on her cheek. They passed and repassed a small herd of elephant. Timothy was hardly frightened at all.

The conversation was not memorable. They were becoming used to each other, and could relax in each other's company. They were full of curiosity about the past and about the present. They did not talk about the future. Constraint there lingered. It occurred to Timothy, for example, to say that they would be well fixed for baby sitters, unless Malvina and the children went back to Los Angeles. But he did not make the remark. It took rather a lot for granted. He was not that much at ease with Catriona. Discussion about having children was for a much later stage.

The aircraft buzzed them again, then wagged its wings. This was the signal that Dieter was satisfied with his footage of the car from the air.

Catriona stopped the car. She sighed. She inspected the grease on her thigh and on Renate's skirt.

She said, 'One thing. If the kids stay in Europe we have plenty of sitters.'

The script, or scripts, laboriously grew. Episode followed startling episode in the amazing journey, or group of related journeys. Timothy's skill in writing dialogue was stretched to, and beyond, its limits. The five versions required styles outside any of his previous performance. The Father was literary, occasionally whimsical, and given to instructional speeches about animal behaviour. The Old Lady was pawky: Timothy based her dialogue on indistinct memories of Dickson McCunn. The Young Lady's plucky lines had something of Dornford Yates, something of the early film rôles of Celia Johnson. The Boy was out of clean cut school yarns; the alluring snare of earlier models, of *The Fifth Form at St Dominic's*, had to be avoided. The Daughter's dialogue was a bowdlerised version of the way the Crombie girls talked. It was much the best because it was genuine.

The different versions made Dieter laugh very much, but the amount of time Timothy spent at his typewriter was displeasing to Catriona.

The dry ice arrived on the supply plane. It was extraordinary how quickly Euan then caused things to move. Dieter bolted one of his cameras to the mount on the door of his Land Rover. Catriona drove the Simca to the track beside the forest. The actors emerged from their quarters looking elaborately unconcerned. Lady Crombie wore a kilt, Kenneth his cap, tie and school blazer. Renate drove Euan's Land Rover to the location. Euan and Kenneth both brought out combs from their pockets and used them, with small, careful gestures, the moment they arrived.

Euan and Dieter had decided not to attempt the in-car shots on this occasion. They could be done at any time and almost anywhere: an out-of-focus background of trees was the only continuity requirement. The thing was to use the dry ice while its virtue lasted.

Euan got behind the wheel of the Simca. He tried to place his artistes in the set. But there were immediate disagreements about who went where. This was the drawback to having so many different scripts. It was at once clear that while Mrs Morgan-Evans and Kenneth knew about each other's versions, and Morag knew about all the versions, neither Euan nor Lady Crombie suspected versions other than their own.

Dieter, who had a camera on a tripod near the Simca, suggested that they try the scene a number of different ways.

'Why?' asked Lady Crombie and Mrs Morgan-Evans simultaneously. They both looked surprised at becoming allies. They glanced at each other. The alliance was terminated.

Mrs Morgan-Evans drew a compact from her shopping bag. She examined her face with satisfaction.

Lady Crombie had a drink from her flask, which she carried on a webbing sling round one shoulder.

Renate got the dry ice in its insulated container from the back of Dieter's Land Rover. She and Catriona made ready to put it in the radiator of the Simca. It was now urgent that Euan should exercise control of the situation.

Lady Crombie said, 'I always liked the front of a car best. I used to beg, when I was a tiny, to be allowed to sit in the front with the chauffeur. My father had the first car in Perthshire. Of course there was usually a liveried footman beside the chauffeur. Or a groom in a cockaded hat. Sometimes both. My father did things properly. They were spacious days, those of my youth. I do not claim that they were perfect. There was much wrong with the world in the years before the Kaiser's war. There was far too much poaching, for example. My great-uncle used to feed poachers to his wolfhounds, until they ate one with a contagious disease. Poor Willie changed all that. Kaiser Bill we used to call him, a dreadful man but I used to admire his helmet. He had a striking line in helmets. Pickle-bottles they were called.'

'We always put up our own pickles at the Clock,' said Mrs Morgan-Evans. 'Big jars we used, with rubber rings inside the lids. Our still room was one of the secrets of our success. Our preserves were quite as good as bought ones. Many people used to mistake our quince marmalade for a bought one. They asked if we shopped at the Home and Colonial. Imagine. My Gareth and I had many a hearty laugh about that. I love laughter. My keen sense of humour has helped me through the bad times as well as the good. Very often, if you look close, you will see the silver lining in the blackest cloud.'

'Perhaps, Mummy,' said Euan, 'if we tried it first with you in the back seat and Rags here beside me—'

'Hoots toots,' said Lady Crombie. She started to climb into the front seat.

The dry ice was now unpacked. It was steaming, as promised, most effectively.

Lady Crombie was a third of the way into the car when her seat was occupied, at the same moment, by Morag and Kenneth. They had climbed over from the back. They began to fight, in silence but with appalling ferocity. There were cries of dismay from some of the adults present; Euan, intervening, was bitten on the hand. Morag was a much better fighter than Kenneth; quite soon he was on his back on the hard ground beside the car. He was blubbering. His tie was under one ear; one sleeve of his blazer was torn away from the shoulder; his hair was not tidy.

Mrs Morgan-Evans swooped on Morag. She tried to drag the child from the front of the Simca. She was perhaps motivated by vengeful love for her damaged child, perhaps by desire to occupy, herself, the seat beside the driver. Morag bit her. At this point Lady Crombie, who had withdrawn, advanced. She hit out with her thumbstick and with her flask. Her motives were also obscure, or mixed; she was driven perhaps by love for a threatened grandchild, perhaps by other demands. It was worth remembering that she had made the first assault on the coveted seat, which, if successful, would have excluded Morag as effectively as her other rivals. She hit Mrs Morgan-Evans on the side of the head with the flask, and jabbed at her backside with the thumbstick. The thumbstick broke. Its splintered end, still jabbing, tore the seat of Mrs Morgan-Evans's safari trousers. They were flimsy trousers, garments of *après safari*; shredding, they revealed a white rubber girdle at which the thumbstick jabbed in vain. Lady Crombie was by this time inadvertently standing on Kenneth. Catriona pulled her off. Renate and Dieter between them pulled Mrs Morgan-Evans off Morag. Morag was left in possession of the battlefield. She was panting, and bleeding from Mrs Morgan-Evans's fingernails, but looked in general much as she always looked; she was an active child, often breathing hard after some burst of exertion, often scratched about the face by thorn or sister.

'Roll,' said Morag to Dieter.

Dieter glanced at Euan. Euan nodded. He was sucking his injured finger, but removed it from his mouth for the camera. He did not take out his comb again, but smoothed his hair back, gently, with the palms of his hands.

Morag visibly tensed. She was about to act.

Dieter started the motor of his camera.

'There is no more any steam,' said Renate. 'The dry ice is melted.'

Neither Mrs Morgan-Evans nor her son appeared at dinner. A bottle of gin and a bowl of fruit were carried to their banda.

Lady Crombie and Morag seemed unaffected by the events of the afternoon. The one talked, the other ate, as usual.

Dieter was depressed. He had spent a long time on the radio telephone trying to get more dry ice flown out from Nairobi, but there was no more to be had.

Renate was also subdued. She told Timothy that she blamed herself, as the multiplicity of screenplays had been her idea. Timothy agreed, but pretended not to do so, as he had caught from Renate the habit of excessive politeness.

Malvina and Grizelda were a bit sour, because they had missed seeing Mrs Morgan-Evans's pants ripped off in the fight.

Euan was in a trance.

Euan unexpectedly joined the party by the fire after

dinner. Adversity, he said, had re-awoken his thirst, which was not dead, as he had supposed, but dormant.

He said, 'Phyllida is in a difficult mood. She declares her intention of bringing an action against my mother for assault. She requires my full co-operation in the matter, asserting that she now has first claim on my loyalty. She threatens to break off the engagement unless she receives my unqualified support, and will certainly withhold from me those privileges upon which, as her betrothed, I have come to rely.'

'I think Rags ought to sue Mrs Morgan-Evans,' said Timothy.

'That is a deplorable suggestion,' said Euan. 'I beg you not to put it into Morag's head.'

He drank off a large neat whisky in the bold manner of his mother.

He said, 'Kenneth, in turn, might sue Rags, for the destruction of his jacket. I might sue Kenneth for the damage to my finger, assuming that Kenneth's teeth were responsible for the indentations which, in a better light, I should be pleased to show you. Whom shall my mother sue? Perhaps Timothy, whose deviousness in the matter of the scripts may justly be held the cause of the fracture of her beloved stick. All these cases will be heard in Nairobi, before a black judge and a black jury, for whom the evidence will be translated into Swahili by an interpreter who will have been bribed by some, or all, of the parties.'

Timothy realised that Euan spoke in jest. This had not all at once occurred to him, as Euan was not given to jokes. He neither made them himself, nor laughed at those made by others. He did not notice them. Tonight whisky, or disaster, induced in him the mood for those cumbrous fantasies.

'What do we do now?' asked Timothy.

'Which of us do you mean by "we"?' said Euan. 'You yourself will no doubt proceed with the seduction of my eldest daughter, a subject to which you and I must return at a more propitious time. Dieter and Renate will retire to their luxurious if overcrowded quarters, there to indulge in practices which I wish neither to hear about nor even to imagine. I myself would repair as usual to my fiancée's cabin, but I doubt if she will be in the mood. I doubt if I am in it myself. I think I shall have a little more whisky.'

'Is this what you're doing?' asked Catriona. 'Seducing me?'

'Not yet.'

'Euan thinks you are.'

'He's quite right in a way. I am seducing you, but I'm only in the early stages.'

'Will I get less of a gut-ache in the later stages?'

'I hope so, darling.'

'I hope so too. Should we step on it a little?'

'I think we should.'

'Did we do it?' asked Catriona. 'Is that it?'

'Yes.'

'The whole bit? What they talk about?'

'Well, yes.'

'Oh.'

'Did you hate it?'

'No. But it's kind of crude. I mean it's kind of unhygienic. Will I get used to that too?'

'I hope so, darling.'

'It cured the pain in my gut.'

'I thought it might.'

After a long time, during part of which Timothy was asleep in Catriona's arms, she said, 'You know something?'

'What?'

'That gut-ache. It came back. And if there's only the one cure for it ...'

CHAPTER 14

Timothy stood with Euan, at the top of the bank, in glorious morning sunshine. Timothy felt taller and better looking than Euan.

'I cannot understand,' said Euan, 'why you introduced so many characters. That is the root of all our trouble, of all yesterday's unpleasantness. I put it to you that we would be better, far better, to return to the simplicity of our original concept. I give you the title *Babe in the Wood*. Babe, singular. I could hardly be more explicit. I do not want to sound tetchy. You have felt bound to explore, experiment. But I cannot help feeling that a lot of our time has been wasted. These elaborate stories of yours are remote from what I want and what I clearly asked for. Let us have no more of this nonsense.'

'Good.'

'You concur?'

'Of course I concur.'

'Then I the less understand the vagaries of your script, or scripts. Can I take it that you will now write, with all reasonable speed, a screenplay to my brief?'

'Yes.'

'You have given up the idea of leaving us?'

'Yes.'

'The utter lack of faith in the whole project, which twenty minutes ago you expressed in intemperate language —learned, I fear, from my daughters—has evaporated?'

'In part.'

'In sufficiently large part to permit the production of a play? What a lot of P's in that question. How I did spit. I must take care, when being alliterative, to choose a different letter. At least in such bright sunlight, and at least just after breakfast. Well?'

'I forget what it was you asked me.'

'So do I. Let us hope the answer would have been the answer I would have hoped it would be. How gnomic I am after too much whisky.'

'Do we stay after all?' asked Catriona.

'For a bit. If that's all right.'

'I don't care. I'll go where you go. I'll stay where you stay. You know what I am? Possessive, that's what I am. I might get a pain in my gut again. I have to have you around to cure it.'

Lady Crombie said, 'Euan has his head in the clouds. He's lived too long in the south. The Soft South, we call it. It takes an auld Scotch body wi' a heid on her shouldies tae tak' a grippie o' the doggie by the tailie. Euan is what they call an exhibitionist. Always dressing up and brushing his hair, even as a tiny. Most really striking men are the same, or they wouldn't be striking. Auchtermoor dressing up for the Perth Ball is like a flapper getting ready for the Garden Party. The whole castle upside down finding his studs and his kilt-pin. And a fine figure he cuts when it's done. I've seen Euan acting. He knows all about making these films, but when he's acting he's like a piece of wood. No idea of it at all. Now the bairns, Morag and wee Kenneth, they may or may not be actors, but they'll do what Dieter tells them. They'll maybe look bonny enough in the forest.'

'That's true.'

'Ay, or I wouldn't have said it. But it wouldn't do to have just the two of them, grabbing the limelight from each other, fighting a running battle, you see what I mean. Och, we'd a' be sent as daft as dabchicks. There will have to be another person with them. A person as different as possible. As old as possible. Then ye'll hae a grand threesome o' puir wee waifies in yon forest. That is a highly commercial idea, Mr McBairn.'

'But Euan's paying me.'

'Come awa', laddie, you an' me are savin' the mannie frae hissel'.'

Kenneth Morgan-Evans said, 'If you don't mind me saying so, sir, you've made the whole thing a bit too complicated, if you don't mind me saying so. I mean you started off with just Mr Crombie and that awful little girl, and then it grew and grew, sir, and don't you think it got a bit sort of spoiled? But I don't think the little girl would really be frightfully good, sir, because for one thing she hasn't got any proper cheekbones, sir, and her hair is always frightfully untidy, sir, and her clothes are an awful mess. I think she'd have a terrible job in learning her lines, sir, don't you, honestly? So if you don't think it's awful cheek, sir, me making a suggestion, don't you think it would be much the best to have just Mr Crombie and me, sir, and have him killed by the elephant right at the beginning, sir, which is a simply super bit, sir, all my friends will like that bit, sir, and then there'll be just me, sir, alone in that great big jungle, sir, dressed like this, sir, which might be jolly effective, don't you think? I don't mind getting all wet in the storm, or watching the leopards do what the mater and Mr Crombie do.'

Mrs Morgan-Evans said, 'It is quite obvious what you must do, Mr Barnes. Crombie is by all accounts perfectly competent behind the camera, but quite without talent in front of it. That is not his fault. Talent is distributed with an unequal hand. Everybody knows that. If I have more than my share it is a responsibility to be shouldered rather than good fortune to be enjoyed. Although he has behaved disgracefully, I feel an obligation to try to save Crombie from the consequences of his own vanity. Of course his mother must be allowed no part in it at all. I have decided to proceed with my action for assault. My situpon is quite sore and my trousers ruined. They cost over three pounds in Bournemouth and I was wearing them for the first time. She is a violent woman, a public danger. It is small wonder, considering how much she drinks. I have to have a little gin because of my back. It is good for my back. It relaxes the vertebrates. I have not been complaining about my back, and never do, but it gives me constant pain. Little Morag has shown herself quite unfitted to take part in a cinema film. Kim held back yesterday because he is the model of chivalry. Not that I object to tomboys. I was a bit of a tomboy myself. I used to get into all sorts of scrapes. I shall be driving the car with Kim beside me. After I have stopped and taken him into the shade of the trees the elephant charges. Kim will be killed. Of course you must fake that bit if you can. I shall be alone with my grief in the midst of the dreadful jungle. There has been occasion for tears in my life, but I have come smiling through with a high heart. What I have described will make everything much easier for you all. It is lucky for Crombie that I am here.'

Dieter said, 'It was wrong of my wife. She apologises to you. I also.'

'Your poor fingers, so much typing,' said Renate.

'We have decided what we must do. It is the only possible solution. It is by the way an interesting idea. We will discuss it with Euan and convince him. Often we have done so. There will be actors in the film only at the very beginning. One is maybe killed. That is not the important. The important is that there is no car, the car is mashed up. Then there is a person alone, but the person is not an actor. It is the camera. Everything happens not to another person whom you see, but to yourself when you watch the film, isn't it? It has been done before but it has never been done well. We shall do it very well. So there will be no more any fights. The camera will not fight with the exposure meter. It will be very interesting and a new dimension in the art of cinema.'

Bill McDavitt said, 'I've just had a signal from the big boss, old boy. The owner. It puts me in rather a difficult spot. It seems that old Euan hasn't paid his bill for the *last* time he was here. Now I'm given plenty of discretion and I don't *have* to turn you all out. Mollie and me have been hearing quite a bit about this film of yours. It sounds top-hole I must say, but we wonder if you're making quite the best of it. We're not complete clots, you know. I mean, a bloke like me is the ordinary sort of bloke who goes to the cinema. We often do a flick in Nairobi, when we're there. I mean, I'm the kind of bloke you blokes make films *for*. What we like is a good story with plenty of action. And of course it's always a lot more interesting if you have quite a few people. I mean, then there's somebody for everybody, if you get my drift. So what we think is, you ought to have about three cars tooling along. Then it's more of a sort of party. There'll be your Simca. That can go in front if you like. Then I'll be coming behind in the old Land Rover, with one or two of the kids. We can pretend they're my kids, if you like. And then Mollie can burn along behind me in the old Toyota, with a couple of our boys in tribal dress. The Toyota's under wraps at the moment but we'll soon have it on the road. Mollie's very keen to join in the fun. I've never seen her so keen about anything, to tell you the truth. It's quite brought the roses to the old thing's cheeks, and I don't want them taken away again. As a matter of fact all this is really her idea. A cracking good one too, in my humble opinion. I hope you agree, old boy, and tap the old keys accordingly, or we'll have to consider our position in regard to that outstanding account of old Euan's.'

'You still want to stay, darling?' asked Catriona.

It was only the second time she had called Timothy 'darling'. The second time was no less startling and moving than the first. Since they were in Timothy's banda he was able to be startled and moved.

'Somebody might come *in*,' said Catriona.

'Nobody will.'

'Somebody might.'

'Nobody will.'

Nobody did.

'I still think it's unhygienic,' said Catriona. 'But you know what it is?'

'What?'

'It's addictive.'

'I have been talking to the McDavitts,' said Euan, 'at some length. I did not grudge the time, owing to the value and interest of what they were saying. They put an idea to me.'

'And to me,' said Timothy.

'Are you not enchanted? All of a sudden we have a *writer's* picture. Characters of all ages and backgrounds. A pattern of developing relationships among themselves, development of each in the face of danger and discomfort, the chance—I am serious—of a *classic*. How puny our first ideas seem. Who'd be a miniaturist when he can fill a broad canvas? I feel myself a very Frith, peopling Epsom Downs on Derby Day with all the sweepings of London. A very Tolstoy. A very Griffith or deMille. Really I am quite excited.'

When Mollie McDavitt came into the bar before dinner she made a sensation. She had done her hair in a new way. She was smoking a cigarette in a holder.

'Hullo, darlings,' she said to Timothy and Dieter.

Two of the waiters in the dining room, normally boy scouts, were in tribal dress. They looked very fine and savage. They performed their duties, but took, as they did so, circuitous routes from tables to kitchen, so that they passed and repassed Euan.

Euan was in a trance.

'He is crazy,' said Dieter. 'At last he is truly crazy.'

'It is maybe coming for a long time,' said Renate.

'No,' said Timothy. 'He's just being blackmailed.'

'So? Mollie has looked in Phyllida's rondeval? Photographs, maybe?'

Euan joined them. His re-awakened thirst was the more vigorous for its long sleep.

He said, 'I do not wish to discuss the picture. I categorically refuse to do so. I wish to speak to you about a personal matter, Barnes, which touches me as a parent and as a man of honour. I think we are among friends. I *think* we are among friends?'

He looked owlishly at Dieter, who winked.

Euan said, 'Does the fellow suffer from a tic? Why does he lower a concupiscent eyelid, grossly redolent of a kind of movie I have never wished to make? The picture I wish to make is a saga of survival in a savage and hostile environment. Two savage and hostile environments. If we include the river, *three* savage and hostile environments. Who is the writer? Am I the writer? I am not the writer. Let him be the writer. We shall have been writers. Thou art the writer.'

'No I'm not,' said Timothy.

'Are you sure? I was clear in my mind—'

'We're leaving.'

'We?'

'Cat and I.'

'I do not recall having accorded you my personal consent.'

'I do not recall having asked for it. I'm completely fed up with this amateurish madhouse. I am leaving. Since Cat is about to marry me, she is leaving too. I'd like your approval but it won't make the slightest difference to my plans.'

'Oh no no. No no no no. You mustn't do that, Timothy. You mustn't leave now. I must make this picture. You must write it. You can't leave.'

Euan was weeping. In attempting to hide his tears he made them more obvious and more heart-rending. He went a little way away from the fire and stood with his back to them.

Timothy turned to Cat, whose hand he held. He said, 'What do we do, darling?'

She said, 'I don't know. You have to choose.'

Dieter said, 'Stay.'

Renate said, 'Go.'

Timothy said, 'I'll decide in the morning.'

'I'll miss the kids,' said Cat. 'And you'll miss the bread.'

'Never mind that. But the kids are a factor.'

'But I have to leave them sometime. And Mal does more for them than I do.'

'And then there's Euan.'

'Yes.'

'It's very upsetting, seeing a man cry.'

'Don't you cry, darling,' said Catriona. 'Don't you cry.'

'How's your addiction?'

'I'm a slave to it.'

Euan said that the picture would start with himself in a brief non-speaking rôle before the main titles, and would thereafter have Rags as its only human character.

'The bill here?' asked Timothy.

'Oversight, not poverty, caused that situation. I have already put the matter right by a call on the radio telephone. This eliminates the McDavitts and their retainers from the cast.'

'Your mother?'

'I shall be firm with her. If she wants to make a film about herself, she can put up the money and hire the crew. I shall send her back to Nairobi, if necessary. To *Scotland*, if necessary.'

'Your fiancée?'

'It is not at the moment clear if that word applies. Nor if Phyllida and her boy will be staying here.'

'If they do stay, and if you are engaged—?'

'Neither will take part in the picture.'

'Is that an absolutely firm and permanent decision?'

'It is a promise.'

On this basis Timothy agreed to stay and to write the screenplay on the original lines.

In return, Euan gave his blessing to the forthcoming marriage of Timothy to Catriona.

CHAPTER 15

Timothy wrote:

1. EXT. PLAIN AND FOREST. DAY 1.

AERIAL SHOT of wide expanse of awesome African plain and lush riverine forest.

TIGHTEN to establish track. A small new Simca car goes slowly along it.

CUT TO

2. EXT. TRACK (MOVING CAR SHOT). DAY 2.

FATHER and DAUGHTER. He driving, she beside him.

FATHER is tall, middle-aged, tanned, greying, wears normal tropical clothes.

DAUGHTER is 12. She has long, untidy fair hair; wears jeans and T-shirt.

The elephant hears them. Father sees the temperature gauge. He reacts to it. He stops the car, gets out, opens the bonnet. Steam gushes. He shrugs to his daughter, smiles ruefully. He leads her towards the trees. They sit down in the shade. No word is spoken. Elephant, car, scream, death. Death obscured by foliage, since shot from daughter's P of V.

The screenplay flowed easily and with marvellous rightness. The storm sequence. The leopards. The hunting dog and the wildebeest. It was good. Timothy knew it was good. He wrote with confidence because he knew the locations, he knew the perils, he knew the star.

Lady Crombie, Mollie McDavitt, Kenneth Morgan-Evans, Bill McDavitt and Mrs Morgan-Evans came to his table by the river, in that order, separately, during the day. The two boy scouts, still in tribal dress, came also, but as neither spoke English their visit was friendlier.

The most distressed of the visitors was Bill. He upset Timothy, because his motives were unselfish. He was the easiest to get rid of.

'I am a hired hand,' said Timothy to them all. 'I'm writing what I am paid to write. This is not my decision. Whether I agree with it or not is immaterial. It is useless to go on at me about it. Now I am afraid you must excuse me as I have a great deal of work to do.'

He said this to the tribesmen as clearly and loudly as to the others. They grinned cavernously, used sign language to beg cigarettes, and went away at last. They thought they were in the film.

'We don't need any dry ice,' said Cat. 'We never did need it.'

'Then how do we get the effect of steam?' asked Timothy.

'With steam.'

'You mean we make the car boil?'

'Sure.'

'We maybe burst it,' said Dieter. 'It will seize up.'

'No. I drive out there, okay? with plenty of water in the radiator. I take plenty more water in a bottle. When you want to shoot the steam, I drain the radiator. But I leave just a little water. Then I run the engine.'

'That is okay,' said Dieter. 'If we are careful. And if we remember to bring more water for the journey back.'

'You could record the noise,' said Timothy to Renate. 'The gurgle and the hiss.'

'No,' said Renate. 'We make better noise in the recording studio.'

Euan did not join them by the fire after dinner. He had lost his thirst with the return of optimism. His mood of despair had passed. He was very pleased with the script, and suggested only small modifications, with some of which Timothy agreed.

'You're clever,' said Timothy. 'Competent. Inventive. Practical. Ingenious.'

'Am I?' said Catriona.

'Thinking of the steam. Thinking it all out.'

'That kind of stuff is my bag,' said Catriona. 'Mechanical stuff.'

'You've made the whole opening sequence work. You've made it possible. The others would have waited about for dry ice until we all grew long white beards. Not you. I don't mean you would have grown a long white beard. Perhaps not Renate.'

'You know something?'

'What?'

'You talk too much.'

'Is that better?'

'Yes, that's better.'

The crew went out as quietly as possible in the middle of the morning. They could not be secretive, since the cars were parked by the office, but they tried to be casual.

Timothy went with Cat in the Simca. Euan and Rags went with the Bruckners in their Land Rover.

They came to the place of the small cow elephant, and of the Battle of the Front Seat. No reference was made to the battle.

Cat got underneath the Simca and unscrewed the plug of the radiator. All the water gushed out. She screwed up the plug again, and put a little water back in the radiator from a plastic jerrican; she said it was enough to make steam, and enough to stop the car seizing up. She knew what she was doing. She got very dirty doing it.

Renate made a careful note of Euan's clothes, which must be matched for the in-car scenes to be shot later, and of Rags's, which would deteriorate during the action but must not in other ways vary. She had already noted the number, colour, model and year of the Simca, and the visible options it sported, such as its radio antenna.

Renate put a little make-up on the scratches which Mrs Morgan-Evans had dug in Rags's cheek and forehead. The scratches were not out of character, but it would be difficult to match them for the in-car shots.

Dieter's first shot was of the car, immobile on the track, from a little way away. Euan rehearsed getting out of the car, walking round to the front, opening the hood. Morag rehearsed sitting still and watching him. They were perfectly satisfactory, once Euan had mastered the trick of undoing the catch of the hood. The rehearsal made Catriona giggle, but it was taken seriously by the others. Timothy was impressed with a feeling of professionalism. He thought the story was in good hands.

Cat started the Simca. She let the engine run. After a short time the small amount of water circulating round the engine began to boil. She got out of the car quickly. She shut the hood, and went back behind the camera.

Euan and Rags got into the car. Renate gave Rags's make-up a quick check.

'Roll.'

'Rolling.'

Renate operated a simplified clapper-board.

'Action.'

The idea, his own idea, was for Euan to switch off the ignition, get out of the car, go round to the front, and open the hood, all as quickly as possible. He was not to waste time acting. He said so himself. He followed this procedure in rehearsal. But now that the camera was rolling a change came over his performance. It expanded in scope and length. He switched off the ignition with a dramatic flick of the wrist, as though despatching an intercontinental ballistic missile. He sighed elaborately, as though in contemplation of a good job done. He gave Rags a quizzical smile, which was not in the script. He got out of the car quite quickly, but his walk round to the front was slow, graceful, and intensely self-conscious. He opened the hood, fumbling a little, as though excitement had made him forget how to do it.

'Cut.'

'Okay, Dieter?'

'Okay with me,' said Dieter. He winked at Timothy.

They did it three more times. By the fourth take Euan was expanding his opening gambits, with key, wrist and smile, to ludicrous lengths; but he made better time over the ground from driving-seat to front.

'I cut it,' said Dieter softly to Timothy. 'I top and tail the shot, isn't it? We have the walk only. Is fine. We print two and four.'

'Two and four,' said Renate, making a note on her clipboard.

The camera came in close to the front of the car. The angle was approximately Rags's point of view but the distance less. Euan was to look up from the steaming innards of the car, shug, grin ruefully at the camera.

'Roll.'

'Rolling.'

'Action.'

Euan looked up as though from a microscope through which he had discovered a new bacillus. He shrugged like Raimu, like Fernandel, like Maurice Chevalier. His rueful grin was amazing. With part of his face he observed the instructions of the script with regard to 'grin', with the rest he fulfilled the requirement of ruefulness; the result was a contortion of features like no expression Timothy had ever seen him adopt.

They did it four more times, and covered the shot from a different angle.

'Is fine,' murmured Dieter. 'A little piece from each shot. A piece of the shrug, a piece of the smile.'

They went to a reverse-angle shot: Rags responding to her father's grin and scrambling out of the car. Rags's grin was pretty good. It was the family smile, broad and sweet. It was affectionate, understanding, forgiving, trusting. She scrambled out of the car like a little girl scrambling out of a car.

Cat looked at the car to see if she could fill up the radiator. She said that it was still far too hot for her to risk doing so.

Dieter moved his camera to a place midway between car and trees. He pointed it away from the trees, out over the enormous plain which he had already photographed from the air.

Renate checked Rags's make-up.

Timothy and Cat went to the edge of the forest and sat down in the shade. They kept behind the camera. They sat close together, holding hands. Their thighs were pressed together.

'Trouble is,' said Cat, 'it's like cigarettes.'

'What?'

'When I want a cigarette I just have to have one. It doesn't happen all the time. I don't smoke all that much. I can go for two–three hours without thinking about it. But when I *want* one I *want* one.'

'I do too,' said Timothy.

'Now?'

'Yes. Now.'

'Can we?'

'No.'

'No. Addiction is a terrible thing.'

Dieter shot a dozen takes of Euan and Rags walking hand in hand from the car towards the camera. Euan's walk was the trouble; it was inconsistent; sometimes he strode forward as though to avenge his daughter's dishonour, Rags trailing behind like a piece of bunting; sometimes he ambled; sometimes he looked about alertly; sometimes he was in a trance.

Dieter thought a short piece of one of the takes would be all right.

This was the moment for the cutaway, perhaps the third, of the alert but amiable elephant.

The cut back was to show Euan and Rags sitting down in the shade. The hiding place for Rags was nearby; it had been chosen weeks before.

Cat had another look at the car. It was still far too hot to refill. Cold water would crack the cylinder head. But there was plenty of time.

Dieter and Euan were setting up the shot when the sound of an engine came from the south. It grew louder as a vehicle laboured along the track at the edge of the forest. Timothy and Catriona looked at each other. Dieter and Renate looked at each other. Morag looked at her father. Euan looked inwards at his thoughts.

A Land Rover bumped into sight round an outcrop of the forest, an untidy peninsula of rank vegetation encroaching on the arid plain owing to a bend in the invisible river. Bill McDavitt drove the Land Rover, which was his. Mollie sat beside him. Two of their boys were in the back. They stopped immediately behind the Simca, not a yard separating bumper from bumper. They all got out. Bill was dressed normally. The two Africans were the boy scouts who had reverted, or graduated, to tribal finery. They grinned at Timothy, who was their friend. Mollie was smoking with her cigarette holder; she was dressed for a ladies' charity coffee morning.

All four advanced towards the edge of the forest.

Bill said, 'I thought I ought to tell you, Euan old chappie, that I've had another signal from the big boss in Nairobi. That's an awful tarradiddle you told me about the bill being paid. Shame on you. Mind you, I'm not saying you did it deliberately. I'll always give an old friend the benefit of the doubt. The fact is you owe the company for the last visit, which as you remember was quite a gang of you for quite a spell. We can stretch a point, old boy, but we're not running a charity. You know that as well as I do. However I don't intend to turn nasty about it. I hate unpleasantness. We both do. They give me quite a bit of discretion. Lucky really, isn't it? What it all adds up to, old boy, is that I'm prepared to trust you. Not you so much as the profitability of this movie of yours. We've heard all about it, you know. Not eavesdropping. We couldn't help it. But we don't think there's much future in the way you're going about it. I don't say Morag isn't a grand kiddie. But what you need is more people in the story, all sorts of different people. We've talked about it a lot. It's obvious, when you come to think about it. The more people you have, within reason, the more people you get interested in it. My commanding officer here will interest all kinds of people. She always interests me, and I'm an average kind of bloke. And the African boys here. How are you going to interest an African audience without African characters? It stands to reason. I can't imagine why you didn't think of it yourselves. I wouldn't dream of dictating to you, old boy, but you do see how we're fixed. I've got an obligation to the big boss. He gives me some discretion. I have to assess whether the film you make is going to pay our bills. I don't *want* to, I've got to, twig?'

Euan did not reply. He looked incapable of replying.

Mollie said, 'You can all hide behind those trees while I pretend to distract the elephant.'

Into a heavy silence came the sound of another engine.

The sound grew louder much more quickly than had the sound of Bill's Land Rover. The new vehicle was being driven much faster: much too fast for the nature of the ground. It tore round the outcrop of forest, skidding and bumping wildly. Lady Crombie was at the wheel. She was driving Euan's Land Rover much faster than Cat ever drove it except on the best metalled roads. Beside her, clinging, sat Mrs Morgan-Evans. Kenneth Morgan-Evans was in the back. He was bouncing up and down on the back seat like a novice on a trampoline. The Land Rover skidded to a halt, cannoning lightly into the McDavitts' Land Rover. There was a moderate clang; Mrs Morgan-Evans and her son were thrown backwards in their seats. They got out. Lady Crombie was dressed in kilt and Tam o' Shanter. Her flask was slung round her neck and she had a small cigarette in her mouth. Mrs Morgan-Evans was in pinkish khaki; her broad-brimmed hat was tied under her chin with a veil. Kenneth was in school uniform; he wore his cap; his blazer had been repaired. He was very neat, in spite of his rough ride in the Land Rover.

They advanced towards the edge of the forest. Peace had been made between Lady Crombie and Mrs Morgan-Evans. They had sunk their differences in a common cause.

Lady Crombie said, 'Ye thocht tae sneak oot o' the policies intil the woods, eh ma mannie? We'll no hae siccan thievish ploy. Phyllida and I have come to a decision between us, Euan dear, with which, in the end, you are quite sure to agree. Mr McBairn will of course then do as you tell him. Is that my granddaughter's hand you are holding, Mr McBairn? I mind my uncle Jamie once, Sir James McQueen of Cailzie, caught a laddie squeezing the fingers of his daughter. She was another Catriona. He out with his skean dhu and chopped off the man's nose. It fell to the ground at their feet and a tomcat made away with it to the stables. "I'll teach you to sniff at your betters,"

Cailzie cried. The lass was concerned about the tomcat, knowing the man had a cold in the nose and the germs might be carried to the horses. Her own horse began to cough a week later, so she had the rights of it. It was entered at the Perth races, too, so their ante-post bets were down the drain. Let that be a lesson to you.'

Mrs Morgan-Evans said, 'I have decided to let bygones be bygones and to save you all from yourselves. Anybody else in my position would be rancorous, and cherish a grudge. But that is not in my nature. It is only the immature spirit which is unwilling to forgive. The older soul recognises that inferior creatures cannot always help themselves. Allowances must be made. The cinema film as we have planned it will be a great success. People will flock to see it. It will be the making of you all. You will thank us in years to come.'

Kenneth Morgan-Evans's lips framed, soundlessly, the words: 'Years to come.'

Bill McDavitt said, 'I don't know precisely what your plans are, old thing, but I'm jolly glad to see you here just the same. The more the merrier. I've been telling old Euan here that we need all hands to the pumps to get this flick off the ground.'

Mollie said, 'There is plenty of room for you all to hide behind the trees while I save your lives from the elephant.'

Timothy still had hold of Catriona's hand. It was his guide and talisman; he did not want, or intend, ever to let go of it. Catriona's hand gave his a sharp squeeze. He glanced at her, smiling. She was looking fixedly to her left, her mouth open. Timothy followed her gaze.

An elephant came into view round another small outcrop of forest.

This was not one of the small cows which they had seen in this place on the day of their arrival. It was not small, nor a cow. It was a very large old bull elephant with huge, asymmetrical tusks.

Dieter said quietly, 'Everybody must be absolutely silent. Do not move or make any noise.'

A light wind was blowing from the elephant towards the people at the edge of the forest. The elephant would not catch their scent unless the wind changed. The people were all in the shade of the trees; if they were motionless the elephant might not see them. But it had very keen senses. Dieter was right. Movement or sound would be very dangerous indeed.

The elephant seemed bored. He had nothing on his mind. He was underemployed. He was not in a mood to browse on the trees or to take a bath in the river.

He saw the Simca and the Land Rovers. The sun glared off the windows and the bright new paint of the Simca. The elephant's great ears twitched and he gestured delicately with the tip of his trunk. The bonnet of the Simca was still open so that the breeze would cool the overheated engine.

The elephant walked very slowly towards the cars. He was in no hurry. He had all day and nothing to do. There was no expression on his face; his air expressed a bored curiosity. He was coming to investigate the cars as a way of passing the time.

He came up to the Simca. He waved his trunk in languid greeting, like a Regency exquisite in the window of White's. He was interested, perhaps, in the unfamiliar exhalations of oil and rubber and gasoline. He waved the delicate, prehensile tip of his trunk over the uncovered engine of the Simca. His curiosity was mildly aroused. He wanted to make friends. He towered over the glossy little car, the intriguing but undemonstrative stranger whose better acquaintance he had decided to make.

He lowered the tip of his trunk. His movements were gentle. His manner told the car not to be frightened; it invited a friendly response.

He recoiled, trumpeting. He screamed at the betrayal.

The hot metal of the Simca's engine had hurt and enraged him. He was very angry indeed. He lowered his tusks and tossed the Simca on to its side and then on to its roof. He knelt on it. There was a tremendous rending of metal and explosion of glass. He set about the Simca with knees, feet and tusks. He was trumpeting incessantly. The noise of demolition excited him further.

He turned from the Simca to the Bruckners' Land Rover. He knocked it on to its side and set to work. It was stronger than the Simca but it was not nearly as strong as the elephant.

He crushed Euan's Land Rover, then returned to the Simca.

Soon the wreckage of the vehicles was spread over a wide area. The elephant addressed himself to the slow, laborious task of flattening each piece of metal to a depth of a few inches.